Dennis Cooper lives in Los Angeles. One of America's fore-most writers, he is also the author of two novels, *Frisk* and *Closer*, and a collection of short stories, *Wrong*, all of which are published by Serpent's Tail.

Dennis Cooper

Try

I'm very grateful to Walt Bode, Jesse Bransford, David Ehrlich, Mark Ewert, Amy Gerstler, Matt Greene, Michael Matson, Ira Silverberg, Mitchell Watkins.

First published in 1994 by Grove Press, New York

I Apologize is based on *Raised by Wolves*, a great and similar zine out of New Mexico, edited by Mr. Ed.

The epigraph is from Robert Bresson, *Notes on Cinematography* (New York: Urizen Books, 1977).

Hüsker Dü quotes: p. 6, from the song "Celebrated Summer," on the LP *New Day Rising* (SST Records); p. 11, from the song "59 Times the Pain," on the LP *New Day Rising*; p. 21, from the song "I Apologize," on the LP *New Day Rising*; p. 100, from the song "Everything Falls Apart," on the LP *Everything Falls Apart and More* (Rhino Records).

Slayer quotes: p. 15, from the song "Cleanse the Soul"; p. 25, from the song "Silent Scream"; p. 58, from the song "Cleanse the Soul"; p. 73, from the song "Live Undead"; p. 115, from the song "Cleanse the Soul"; p. 116, from the song "Spill the Blood." All songs from the LP *South of Heaven* (Def Jam Recordings).

The right of Dennis Cooper to be identified as the author of this work has been asserted by him in accordance with the Copyright, Designs and Patents Act 1988

A CIP record for this book is available from the British Library on request

This edition first published in 1994 by
Serpent's Tail, 4 Blackstock Mews, London N4

Printed in Great Britain by Cox & Wyman Ltd., Reading, Berkshire *for Casey*

The thing that matters is not what they show me but what they hide from me and, above all, *what they do not suspect is in them.*

—Robert Bresson

Ziggy's splayed in bed editing *I Apologize*, "A Magazine for the Sexually Abused." Four or five copies have sold at this cool, mainly CD-cassette store where Calhoun, his best friend, works part-time. This'll eventually be *I Apologize* No. 20. Last time Ziggy checked it was 1:37 A.M. At the moment he's hunched over, filling up most of page eight with a self-portrait. Him scared. Not bad considering the nothing technique. Tick, tick, tick, tick . . . When Ziggy thinks his depiction's okay, i.e., now, he moves the pencil to a different locale on the page, gradually clogging this straggly figure's surroundings with words. *Don't panic get a grip you don't have to sleep if you don't want to.* They're twisting and winding all over the fucking place. Very . . . psychedelic? "Hm." Weird how professional it looks. Last weekend, scribbling that sentence on a loose scrap of homework, he'd felt like "auditioning for a snuff film," as Uncle Ken joked one time.

"Shit." He owes that old psychotic a call. 1:59 A.M. He pushes the part-finished zine aside, looking worriedly at a Polaroid he based the self-portrait on. It shows Ziggy shirtless, in cutoffs, head turned, eyeballing Calhoun before a bad thrift-store painting of Paris, face charged by a happy if slightly hysterical expression. Calhoun just looks . . . high, period. I'm handsome enough, Ziggy thinks. Definitely. Yeah, but . . . His body's just sort of there. Neck down he could be, oh, sixty percent of the guys at his high school. Maybe *he'd* fuck himself if he was sure he was gay, but his taste in men is notoriously primitive, so . . . does that count? "Shit, shit . . ." Ziggy squints at Calhoun for a second, then flicks the Polaroid at the small table next to his bed, where it joins a black push-button telephone, the colorful if empty cassette case for Hüsker Dü's *New Day Rising* LP, and a freshly rolled, unlighted joint. 2:04 A.M.

*A*cross town, Calhoun sits in his fake-antique desk chair injecting a huge dose of heroin. Nearby, a laptop computer's screen exudes this turquoisey glow, into which a paragraph of his novel-in-progress dissolves, or appears to. He unties his arm, blinks, and a subsequent rush, though it's more like an ease—warm, slightly sensual, trancy—cross-fades the world around him into a vague, distant backdrop as well as it can, for a few minutes anyway. That would be the scariest sight in the world—

gentle, brilliant Calhoun and his writing in deep hibernation—but no one else sees. And to him, heroin's perfection or whatever. Calhoun's friends couldn't understand what he's experiencing right now, although one, maybe two of the people he knows worry almost incessantly, even melodramatically at times, irritating him when they announce their concern, since, to his mind, that "concern" is selfserving and thoughtlessly aimed. Take Josie, Calhoun's long-distance girlfriend, whom he keeps half-abreast of his goings-on. She, Ziggy are neurotic as shit about the subject of heroin. Still, they're the people who "love" him. They say so at least, far too often in fact, for whatever that's worth. Calhoun's slightly inscrutable, even to those select few who detect how kind and gifted he is behind an initial remoteness. Whatever, folks. He just wants to feel bliss via heroin. If his friends feel like hanging around with him anyway, fine.

*A*cross town, Ken, Ziggy's overweight uncle, was sitting around making ultra–eye contact with Robin, a thirteen-year-old Heavy Metal fanatic.

"Nice place," the kid said, eyeing the man's stupid furniture and shit.

"Check it out," answered Ken. He heaved-ho his huge body out of the faded green armchair.

Robin stood, followed the man around.

Room, room, room . . . room.

"Here's where I make porno videos." It was a brightly lit room with a set. Outdated motel interior, it seemed. "Maybe we'll make one," he added.

The kid snorted.

"Maybe . . . soon," said the man. He reached out, squeezed the drooping seat of Robin's tattered black jeans.

Un-fucking-believable-looking kid.

"No, let's get really, really, really stoned first." Robin laughed, very jittery. "You know . . . 'cos . . ."

So they traipsed off to the couch.

Ken's big blanched hand with two tiny blue UFOs jammed in the sweaty palm. "Take both," he said.

The kid pried them out, filled his mouth, felt around in a pocket, and traded the man a cassette of his favorite band Slayer's most recent LP.

Cover art: huge, rotting skull populated by demonic, half-human figures.

"Looks good," Ken said, not really thinking that.

"Fuck, I *worship* them, man!" Robin brought a beer can to his mouth.

"To their health." The man smirked. And he raised his own beer.

Both of them: "Glug, glug, glug . . ."

Safely inside the kid's guts, pills began to dissolve, meaning Ken could relax, right? He idly studied the Slayer art.

"Put it *on*," insisted Robin.

"What, this?" Ken asked. He held up the ugly cassette case.

Excited kid's brown bordering on reflective black eyes.

"H-hello?" Nicole's voice is sort of, uh, vague, à la Calhoun's, though, fingers crossed, it's just drowsiness, and not . . . whatever . . . heroin?

"It's me," Ziggy says into the phone. "Ziggy McCauley. Uh, who always wears a jeans jacket?"

"Oh, hi-i-i." She yawns, a lengthy, multipitched type. Even thinned to a wisp by the mechanism, the sound's totally erotic.

"Hi."

Yawning apparently burned off the cloud since her voice turns a touch . . . crisp. "Ziggy," she says. "How *are* you?"

"I'm okay. Stoned. Uh, you?" He reaches down, wiggles his hardening cock.

"A bit hazy, naturally. Oh, listen, I was thinking about you today."

"Really? Ha ha ha, sure." Ziggy's left foot starts spazzing out, a semiconscious bad habit that just makes him more overwrought, though it's not as if he can adjust it.

She hums a little melody like she's pissed off or

embarrassed to continue. It, the melody, sounds vaguely familiar. Like from MTV, radio. Ziggy narrows it down to a category (rap), and a gender (female), but the tinier details elude him. Shit. "So, what's your opinion of Hüsker Dü?" he interrupts hopefully.

Her song shorts out.

" 'Cos I love them," he adds.

"Mm. I've heard the name."

Ziggy reaches over, pushes PLAY on his cassette deck. *New Day Rising* comes on. "Listen to this. Just for a second, okay?" He holds the receiver to one of the speakers. "Celebrated Summer" happens to be playing. *. . . I summer where I winter, and no one is allowed there . . .* After a minute he hauls the receiver back up to his mouth, yells, "This is so fucking *great,*" then shoves it back into the song for twenty, twenty-five seconds. . . . *Then the sun disintegrates behind a wall of clouds . . .* "Isn't that genius?" Ziggy asks. "No matter what Bob Mould's singing it makes me cry! Not really, but . . . you know what I mean? I hate it that they broke up! Assholes! Not really!" He snickers off "microphone."

"Interesting."

Ziggy turns down the stereo. "They're great."

"I believe you. So what do you do on the days when you don't come to school?"

"Hang out with weird people mostly." Ziggy looks around the room. Crammed with furniture, crammed with books, papers, etc., it's practically a cave it's so craggy and dusty and horribly lit by his desk lamp. "Work on my magazine, uh—"

"Anybody I know?" There's this new little twist in her voice Ziggy can't quite identify other than to guess she's even less out of it than before.

"No, uh-uh," he says. "Well, maybe. You might know this guy Calhoun." She doesn't say anything. "He's my best friend. Then there's this other guy, Ken. He's my uncle, uh . . . stepuncle? I mean, I'm adopted, right? So he's my . . . *one of my* dads' brother, uh . . . 'Cos my parents are two gay men, right?"

"Really? That's . . . unusual." She clears her throat.

"I guess." Ziggy's cheeks have knotted painfully around his big nose the way they do when he's nervous. "Anyway, uh . . . yeah, my uncle's, like, totally psycho, but I happen to dig him. He teaches me stuff. Oh yeah, such as what, she asks? Ha ha ha. Well, about . . . uh, well . . ." A headache's sort of eating his train of thought. *"Well, okay* . . . he's into, uh . . . he's got these kiddie porn videos. You know what those are? He makes them. That's one thing . . . Uh, you still . . . okay?"

Nicole doesn't say anything, but she's obviously there 'cos Ziggy can hear the inside of a house, meaning . . . how to describe it? A kind of textured silence, like that "music" his therapist plays in their background.

"Okay, assuming you're listening, uh . . . Uncle Ken's got all these videos of young boys and him having sex. Even sixteen's too old. Like I'm *completely* over the hill now. But we're friends 'cos he's into the idea of sexual abuse. Me too. I'm a victim, right? Anyway, that's *another* long story. So, based on this, do you think I'm insane?"

Nicole's mouth makes watery noises. Swish, swish, swish . . . "I guess I'm . . ." swish, swish . . . "worried about you. I've been hearing things . . . Not about your uncle . . . but that you're . . . com . . . ple . . ." Her sentence disintegrates into a yawn.

"Complex! That's good, yeah."

"I'm . . . wait . . ." The yawn does its thing. ". . . I'm not judging you, Ziggy," she adds, seemingly composed again.

"Oh, I know. That's okay." He's sure now he really does like her. "I'm definitely weird, Nicole. My main dad—the one I still live with—has been beating me up, raping me since I was, uh . . . ten, and my other dad just wrote me this letter that was like . . . obviously sort of a, uh, love letter, and I guess . . . uh, I wrote one back, and now we're gonna sleep together, which is probably this huge mistake. And . . . what else . . . ?" He pounds his forehead a few times. "But I really do like you. I *do*. I have for a while." He blinks wildly at the cave.

"I . . . like you too."

"What? That's unbelievable!" Ziggy digs a hand into his longish brown hair. It used to be longer. "Can I . . . ? What about this weekend? I'll come see you. I'll hitchhike, *I* don't care." He rolls onto his side and starts pawing the black slice of air that separates his twin bed from the mashed-down shag rug.

"That'd be nice."

"Great!" There's so much dust under the bed it feels slippery. Like his hand's sort of . . . not skiing exactly, but . . . what? "Maybe I'll actually show up at school in the morning and shock everyone." He's still scrounging through invisible books, magazines, videocassettes, papers, stiff towels, etc. "Or . . . I'll call you, okay?" Nicole answers, "That's cool," or whatever. He's too busy hunting down one . . . particular . . . porn magazine. When he finally finds, yanks *Broad Strokes* 7, his hand wears a tangle of dust balls so dense and entwined it's like a glove, or . . . the ghost of a glove, at first glance anyway. Pretty. Blink, blink, blink . . . "Jesus." Shaking his hand, he reduces the grayish white bundle to fiberettes. "Uh, Nicole? I've gotta . . . go. Bye." Ziggy hangs up, snickers down at the magazine's lounging, inexplicably savory cover girl. She could be Nicole's sleazier sister, maybe. Same mousy hair, button nose, close-set eyes. And the coiled snake tattoo on her ass could potentially lurk beneath one of the loose-fitting dresses Nicole tends to wear. So Ziggy closes his eyes and imagines it's postschool tomorrow, Nicole's parents' house, which suspiciously resembles Calhoun's loft since that's no sweat to conjure up. They've been talking and smoking pot. It's cool. They're in a bedroom that looks like Calhoun's . . . oh fuck, and, uh, Calhoun's in the bathroom or something, and . . . Ziggy settles back with the magazine. Flip, flip.

No matter how many thousands of times he's turned these same thirty pages, there's always a detail or two he never noticed before. Such as how in, like, ten of the pictures, another porn magazine's just visible on the woman's night table. The miniature cover of . . . of . . . Ziggy squints . . . *Horny Horsetrainers* shows several androgynous, entangled adults wearing cowboy hats. "Nicole's" potbellied, bearded costar obviously needs this other porn to stay hard or something. Well, women *are* awfully nerve-racking, Ziggy thinks. Or maybe *she* needs porn. "Hm." That makes more sense since her costar's a slug, as far as Ziggy can figure. Anyway, "Nicole's" such a loser who gives a shit *what* she requires? "Cool." All this time, Ziggy's been fingering his humid, squashed asscrack. Once, maybe twice, he has brought those fingers up to his nose for a sniff. Weird, he thinks, sniffing again, how this spicy-gross asshole aroma's so priceless to him, but every girl he's fucked didn't care less, or else they kept their remarks to themselves. Wait, on second thought, girls never bury their noses way in there like gay guys he's fucked usually do. Maybe, Ziggy decides, I'll ask Nicole to, like, spelunk there. Or maybe she'll take that route on her own? The idea's so amazing he flings *Broad Strokes 7* away, squints at a bookcase, and pumps his cock, definitely ready to come. The book spines go unfocused like they're on a movie screen, cross-fading into Nicole's sort of Juliette Lewis–ish face, which Ziggy aims toward his splayed legs, beckons, beckons, then . . . slam-dunks so forcefully her cheeks ripple back to the hairline, bunching

up around tiny, pink ears as if she's . . . whatever, rocket-
ing to Mars? Cool. Ziggy's starting to spurt when he feels
this . . . thing inside his chest, like a lodged rock. "The
emotion bomb," as his school therapist describes it. Sometimes as Ziggy has orgasms, the "bomb" goes off too, and
the shambles that makes of his . . . soul, ugh, isn't worth
a momentary otherworldliness. So, forehead scrunched,
he lets his dribbling cock loose and lies as still as he can.
The "bomb" ticks frenetically under his rib cage. "No,
please," Ziggy sobs, slugs his chest. Now he shuts his eyes,
picturing Calhoun, who's the only human being he's ever
known who definitely gives a half-shit about him. "Cal
. . . houn," he chants very intently, until his friend's
big-nosed, dazed, Irish face blankets his thinking, immense as an IMAX screen. "Th-th-th-thanks," he
squeaks. *No problem, Ziggy.* Slug, slug. When the pain's
down a bit, Ziggy fades-out Calhoun, reaches over, grabs,
lights, starts smoking the joint on his bedside, fascinat-
edly watching his sperm dry, his ballsac unfurl, against a
faint, scruffy Hüsker Dü soundtrack. Sniffle. . . . *59 times
the pain I could never be with you* . . . Tick, tick,
tick . . . With one hand Ziggy fingers the eggy white blobs
hardening up on his belly, almost calm and/or stoned out
enough to successfully snag the telephone with his other.

*W*hen Ziggy called, I was at the Macintosh, Walk-
man cranked, so the phone machine answered. As a rock

journalist, I'm often up late, speed-reviewing some concert from earlier that evening. And it wasn't until my
break several minutes later that I noticed the message
light blinking.

Perhaps a little background is in order. Ahem. I
met Brice McCauley, unemployed hunk, at an Echo & the
Bunnymen concert some sixteen years earlier. We fucked,
got along, and wound up leasing a town house together—
our stab at heterosexual-style bliss. We adopted Ziggy, a
hyperactive, hard-to-place two-year-old, as part of this
experiment. But I found the situation intolerable ere long,
and moved to New York, at which point Ziggy was still a
frantic, irritating toddler.

After ten years of zero contact, I ran into my older,
more beautiful son at a Nomeansno concert on one of my
frequent business trips west, and, ever since, we'd been
slowly reinventing our dad-son relationship, mostly via
letter and phone, with the occasional, briefish visitation as
my travel schedule allowed.

Recently Ziggy had written requesting information
on my sex life, as he was attempting to sort out his own,
and I, being something of a blabbermouth, spelled out my
predilection for teens, even going so far as to specify the
act—rimming—which particularly obsessed me re: them.
Almost instantaneously Ziggy wrote back, claiming his
actual interest in asking had been a snowballing love, of
a sexual/romantic sort, for yours truly, and could we
make love, fuck, etc., at my convenience of course?

I was shocked, but it wasn't as if I hadn't fantasized

similarly over the most recent years, since Ziggy's physical charms combined with our familial closeness—plus our lack of actual blood ties—had made the boy queasily attractive. So I wrote back, detailing my ennui at Ziggy's confession, then ultimately accepting his offer, and adding a multipart footnote, namely that he move to New York, live with me, accept the new post of "lover," keep mum re: our past, thereby legitimizing our love in such a way as to avoid explanations that would inevitably be awkward, even among chums. And I had been waiting anxiously for a reply since a week ago Tuesday.

I immediately phoned Ziggy back. The boy sounded stoned—his natural state, when around me at least—though less stoned than he'd seemed just a few weeks before, thanks, it appears, to the interventions of some sort of post-Freudian, psychoanalytical counselor type at his school. After querying Ziggy about his recent activities, rather too perfunctorily no doubt, I took a deep, noiseless breath and refreshed his memory re: my most recent missive's proposal. Ziggy agreed to the plan in a sweetly put stock phrase or two, then all but begged me to fly out and see him. So I checked my appointment book—Ziggy said Brice would be away for the weekend— and agreed to arrive the next morning, stay a day or two, fully expecting that we'd consummate our relationship and set into motion his transference East.

Throughout this conversation, Ziggy mumbled agreeably in stops and starts—rushed, inarticulate, vague, loosely poetic—a "music" I cherish in all teens, particularly, in this case, emitted by such an impeccable face, which I could even then picture—sleepy-eyed, *cute*, crowned with filthy brown hair, big lips moving a little too rapidly at the opposite extreme of the continent.

Slayer's latest LP crushed and splintered Ken's living-room air.

Robin head-banged mechanically, long hair whipping around.

Ken was stroking the kid's ribby back through his untucked T-shirt.

They were perched on the couch by this point.

"Isn't this great?" Robin asked in the space between songs. He flopped back.

"Yeah," Ken said.

Then the man made his face say, Stop stalling.

Another song cranked up and shut the kid's eyes.

"Yeah, yeah," Ken yelled, sensing wariness. "It's *great!*"

The man's hand, elevated on fingertip, walked down the chest of the kid's T-shirt.

Robin's T-shirt was black with the word *Slayer* printed in red and gold gothic-style letters. Ken tugged it up past the naval. An innie. *White* skin. Really hard not to bury one's lips in it.

"Hey," the kid said, batted Ken's hand away. He laughed.

The man raised the shirt past dime nipples.

"Man." Robin laughed.

The kid's stomach bunched up, which looked great.

Robin was Slayer's head-banging disciple again, lips moving roughly along with the lyrics, which talked about Satan, damnation, human sacrifice, etc.

Dark pink eyelids penciled once above the lashes with liner then brushed very lightly above and below with a cobalt blue powder that looked prostitutey, not fierce, assuming that's what the kid had intended.

Slayer: *Body that rest before me, with every dying breath* . . .

A quarter inch maybe of licorice black roots in Robin's long, yellow, frazzly hair.

Skin that never saw daylight or wouldn't let daylight soak in.

"So I have this idea," said Ken.

Robin snorted. Something . . . the tension made head banging tough, so he quit and flopped back in the cushions again.

"The video," Ken added. He was gathering handfuls of Robin's black jeans, which he yanked to get a look at the hips, butt, thighs. Feeble little things.

Robin's too-made-up eyes looked a third scared and two-thirds too confident.

"You don't mind, right?" Ken asked, yanked.

Glancing away with a slight smile . . . "Barry told me about you," said Robin.

"About the payment too?" Ken yanked.

The kid nodded, then something in Slayer took over his eyes, lips, and he mouthed the line *Stained glass windows black*.

Tick, tick, tick . . .

Robin head-banged awhile.

"Barry's gorgeous," Ken said, just to say something.

*W*hen the heroin filters into Calhoun's bones or wherever, he reaches out, almost too gracefully, thanks to the high, and picks up a videocassette on his TV, which, like most things in the room, is an arm's length away from the desk where he does his shot several times daily. The tape's a homemade porno Ziggy lent him last night. Ziggy wants Calhoun's "brilliant" opinion. So he inserts the cassette in his crap VCR, lighting a Marlboro Light. No credits, obviously. Dead white smoke seeps from Calhoun's open mouth, drifting into his contracted eyes, blink, blink, which are in their unkempt, vaguely coming-down phase. There's a ton going on in them. Rubbing his nose with the back of one hand, he sits up, blinks himself to attention. Okay. There's Ziggy suddenly, for sure, as a kid, naked, flat on his back on a bed somewhere, masturbating a teensy dick. Calhoun cringes and grins at the same time. Tick, tick, tick . . . Hours of someone he'll eventually know having lopsided sex with obese Uncle What's-his-name. No sound. To Calhoun, the video's little

more than this ludicrous joke for a while. Then he either
gets bored or outraged, he can't decide. Fatso endlessly
does shit to Ziggy. It's hard to watch, being so foreign.
Plus it has no momentum, at least to an outsider. And
then there's the issue of Ziggy right there in the thick,
looking off into space or sometimes at the lens with an
early version of that please-love-me squint Calhoun
knows very well and deflects all the time. "Jesus, man."
Calhoun gives a little poke to his crotch, which is as gushy
and lifeless as ever. Then, reassured, he spaces out on, oh
nothing . . . the TV. The porno dissolves into Calhoun's
low opinion of the conventional world. "Phew." People
are viruses, he thinks. Blink, blink. Now he can manage
a wan smile. Click. Ziggy's video rewinds in the distance.
Jesus, heroin helps keep things *so* . . .

Ziggy looks carefully at the pale blue Y his stomach, hips, and widespread legs suggest under the top
sheet. Then he pinches a bit of the sheet between thumb
and forefinger, yanking same to the side. "Presto," he
whispers. A skinny beige body, six chest hairs, extremely
faint tan line, cock and balls symmetrical in a reddish
brown bush. If I was absolutely gay, he thinks, or a
woman, ha ha, *I'd* fuck this body. Okay, well, not *fuck* in
the latter case because *that's* impossible, but . . . what?
Hold, kiss, blow, uh . . . Oh, shit. Ziggy cringes. I just,
like, *agreed* to fucking *move* to *New York* with *Roger!* Shit,

shit, shit . . . He jumps out of bed, rummages through a
desk drawer until he finds the envelope from his less scary
dad. He hops back in bed and pulls the sheet up to his
waist, letter out, already reading. *My Dear Ziggy, The sky
is a malted milk gray out* . . . Blah, blah, blah . . . blah, blah
. . . Here. "This part," Ziggy thinks aloud, gripping the
pages. First Roger's supposedly *more than a little embarrassed to detail my mildly pedophilic interests to you, a young
person yourself* blah, blah, blah . . . Then, let's see . . .
*Teenaged boys are my weakness, particularly the slim, de-
pressed, cute, intelligent, haunted ones who feel askew in
some way from their peers. My interest seems to reinforce
these boys' secret if fragile belief in themselves* . . . Spooked,
Ziggy lets the letter drop on his chest. It folds up into
this . . . "Hm." Well, it looks like a drainpipe. Collapsed.
Starting nowhere, leading nowhere. Actually, it reminds
him even more of those cardboard box lean-tos some
homeless adults have built under the freeway off ramp
near their place. Ziggy stares off, imagining himself all
curled up in a gross-smelling ball inside one of them. Why
aren't there homeless dollhouses? he wonders. Blink,
blink . . . Someone could get megarich manufacturing and
selling them. Maybe Calhoun and him. He can see it. But
the excitement, like, wilts once he grabs and reopens the
letter. This part . . . his eyes narrow, focus a bit . . . *because
you're probably wondering what my exact tastes entail.
Ahem. First of all, understand that my heightened, nitpicky
perceptions of popular music extend to human beings. Thus
I choose friends selectively, and bed partners even more selec-*

*tively still. To me teenaged boys of the sort I have indicated
are an example of human beings at their most fiercely alive,
most . . . evolved, let me say.* Ziggy's crotch feels like it's
falling asleep, bzzz . . . Bad sign, bad sign. *As for what I
like to do with them, rimming's the technical term for it.
"Eating ass" is a lowlier synonym. Do you know that many,
many gay men are more interested in asses than they are in
big cocks, despite all the hype to the contrary?* "Sometimes,
yeah," Ziggy whispers. *I love to spend quality time with a
beautiful teenaged boy's ass, massaging, mapping, recording
its factual data, putting my tongue in the hole (this is a
common gay sex act), fingerfucking it (ditto), and so forth.
Don't think for a moment that this brand of sex has any
relationship at all to the "sex" Brice imposes on you. It's far
more like worship, if anything.* Then the letter apologizes
for being so crass for about half a page. Ziggy skims. He's
already picturing that ass stuff. Tossing the letter away,
he sidelines the sheet, grabs his knees, folds himself up,
card table–style, simultaneously doing a semi–back flip,
such that his ass leaves the mattress and sort of flies open.
Now he strains his green eyes in that basic direction. But
bodies are too crude or sneaky or something. So he settles
back, feeling around as intricately in his asscrack as possible, as if the few hairs and puckered hole were an insignia
or braille. And if they *were* braille, they'd probably say,
"Bye," he thinks, ha ha ha ha. Ziggy shuts his eyes,
daydreaming, fingering, but every time he forms a picture
of Roger's pale, big-featured face smashed to dreck in his
crack, that reasonably sexy portrait starts mutating

. . . or, uh, shape-shifting. Like it's been infected, or
. . . as if its eyes are eyeholes and Brice is spying on him
or . . . *what?* "Shit . . . shit, shit . . ." Ziggy slugs his
mattress with both fists. "I hate you," he says, meaning
Brice, and maybe Roger a little. Squeak, squeak. Ziggy
stands, fumes for a second, then plows into his cramped,
cluttered bedroom, tearing precious Hüsker Dü posters
right off the walls, chucking books, sketch pads, papers,
cassettes every which way. He topples a chest of drawers,
hopping onto its thin plywood back. One foot crashes
through, plunging practically up to the knee in a tangle of
lukewarm underwear and stray socks. That feels . . . sad
for some reason. "Fuck!" Crash. His other foot stomps
through the wood, and is immersed in some T-shirts,
handkerchiefs, etc. They swim around that calf and ankle
like . . . jellyfish or whatever. "Oh, *no*," he says, noticing
the first dim, dim pulse of an idiotic emotion bomb. Dropping into a crouch, he bear-hugs his thighs, wedges a
chunk of his face into the narrow V formed by his
knobbed, parallel knees, and breathes as asthmatically as
possible, trying to sober himself on the lemony stench of
his unshowered crotch. Sometimes that works. "Shit." He
tries berating himself incoherently. But the blubbering's
already started. "Shi-i-i-it . . ." Ziggy's lost in the scarily
complex if amateurish feedback of his feelings. "Shi-i-i-
it." Crunch. The bedroom door flies open, smacking a
wall. Brice, nude, red hair gone volcanic, face a purple and
bellowing splat, sort of careens at him. Ziggy's greasy
brown hair is yanked hard in two spots, and he levitates—

rips, actually—straight up and out of the dresser. "Stop!"
The jagged wood's cutting his ankles to shit, he can tell.
"Dad, *please.*" Ziggy's dragged away, pinned against one
wall, pushpins gouging his back. Blurry Brice knees him
once, twice in the groin, lets his hair go, steps out of the
way. Ziggy can't breathe, gags, gasps, hits the rug, his legs
practically vibrating. He crawls, gently cupping his balls,
helped along by some kicks that smash his flesh into the
crags of his skeleton. The seventh kick lands him across
the dresser. Using one arm, he hugs the piece of furniture.
The other arm, hand swing around his back, trying to
cover his blunt little asscrack. Kick. "I've *seen* your can
before," Brice yells, kicks Ziggy's hand. It snaps so loudly
that something's probably broken inside. Now there's a
relative silence apart from Ziggy's sobbing, obviously, not
to mention the Hüsker Dü album, thank God. Then Brice
snorts and says, "Well, you're the one who has to live in
it," which Ziggy initially thinks means his body. But
Brice probably meant, like, what's left of his bedroom.
Slam. Ziggy's alone again. . . . *All these crazy mixed-up lies
floating all around, making these assumptions brings me
down* . . . He can't seem to move. "Shit." Down the hall,
another door slams. What if I'm paralyzed? he thinks.
Concentrating, he manages to move a thigh, calf very
slightly. Phew. The Hüsker Dü tape's reached his favorite
song, "I Apologize," a raucous, fierce, kind of confused,
pretty rant against the way the world works that's so
appropriate to his current situation it's almost hilarious.
That's why he borrowed the name for his magazine. But

every Hüsker Dü song is relevant to Ziggy's life every second. That's why they mean tons to him now. Along with Calhoun, probably Nicole, maybe Roger, but nobody else . . . well, apart from Annie, who's so generous with her drug supply. Then there's Uncle Ken, ugh, whom he really should phone. "Shit." Raising up, twisting his body around, Ziggy grimaces through the room's ruins at a way tilted digital clock. 3:17 A.M.

Click.

"Ken," announces a whiny male voice, followed by the sound of air whistling in and out of lungs buried underneath at least two hundred eighty pounds of skin, fat, bones. His uncle's definitely more frightening on the phone. In person, obesity suits him somehow. Or Ziggy's used to it. Weird.

"It's *me*," Ziggy says, sniffling. "Brice just beat me up. Can I . . . come over?" He cringes hopefully.

"We-e-ell," Ken answers, voice all wavery, rocked by . . . alcohol? Duh. "I've . . . let me catch my breath . . . got this kid over here. And we're . . . *you* know. So you can come, hang out, crash. But you may see some shit that'll haunt you a little."

Before replying, Ziggy listens to the music blasting distortedly in Ken's background. It's sinister, but dumb. "That sounds interesting, Uncle Ken," he says. "But I'm probably too freaked tonight."

"So what else is new."

"Yeah, right." Ziggy snickers. Then he remembers how Uncle Ken stared at Calhoun the time they stopped by together, and his fingertips start to pulse rapidly. He crosses a couple. "So, who's the kid? Do I know him or her?"

"According to Robin here, he's the world's biggest Slayer fan. Hear music? That's Slayer. Ever heard of them? What else . . . He's about, oh . . . twelve, thirteen. You know those Glam Heavy Metal types? Dyed blond hair, headband, a little eyeshadow, lipstick?"

"God, I hate those kinds of guys." Ziggy's smeary eyes narrow and flit to the garbage-strewn floor, specifically a shred of Bob Mould's honest, middle-aged-before-its-time face.

"Yeah, it's *great*," Ken whines, to the boy in his . . . living room, probably. "I'll be off in a second, okay? Well, if you hate them, Ziggy," he adds, lowering his voice. "You should pop by."

"Tomorrow maybe." Ziggy's picked up the poster scrap. "After school. Will the kid still be there?" Looking into Bob Mould's enlarged, tinted eye, the situation kind of dissolves into a general okayness.

"Yeah, yeah . . . Look, he's getting antsy. Gotta go. No, sit there, Robin. *Sit back down.*"

Click.

The kid tried to stand, but the strange combination of beer and sleeping pills wouldn't let him. So, flop, he fell back on the couch.

"What's the problem?" Ken asked.

Robin slurred.

"What?" Ken repeated, standing over the kid.

On second hearing, the kid said, "Who was that?"

"My nephew," Ken answered, kneeling down by the couch. "The boy's insane." Ken grabbed the waistband of Robin's jeans, yanking them and the underwear all the way off.

"Insane." The kid giggled. He jerked his hips around wildly.

"Ziggy's a closeted homo," said Ken, soaking in Robin's finery.

Then the kid sat head-banging a bit, not that well, he could tell, but . . .

"Get up for a second," the man said.

Robin tried to stand, fell backwards. Again. Forget it. So the man helped him down to the rug, where he knelt, teetering, long blond hairs glued to his cute, sweaty face.

Ken unfolded the couch bed, then watched the kid teeter awhile.

"Heave ho," announced the man, clutching a thin wrist.

Robin landed face down on the bed and sort of squirmed while Ken French-kissed his not-that-clean buttcrack. Sometimes he sang along with Tom Araya, Slayer's vocalist, who was yelling about how Christianity's a lie and Satanism's perfection.

"Let's make that video," Ken said. He could taste Robin's shit kind of generally. "Up, up," he added, and slapped the flushed butt.

Robin tottered into another room.

Light.

"Wow." The kid gasped, hid his eyes. "Man, that's intense." He could see a camera. The motel-looking bed. Ken way off to the left, naked, fat. "But . . . I don't know," he added.

"All right, *three* hundred dollars."

"Creep," Robin whispered.

Slayer, lyrics and all, barreled right through the walls, luckily for Robin.

Gripping that thin wrist again, Ken whipped the gyrating kid at the "bed." Robin stumbled there, fell on it.

Ken stood looking down at the crooked, white butt. Sweet, he thought. Its perfection made Robin-nobody a magnet. How?

"I'm gonna fuck you," said Ken.

"But," Robin slurred. And his butt tensed. He was thinking of AIDS, which he didn't know that much about.

"Then we'll rest."

Shutting his eyes, Robin silently asked Tom Araya of Slayer to help him relax.

Slayer: *Restrained insane games suffer the children condemned* . . .

The kid's butthole gulped down Ken's cock, wiping both of them out.

"Stop!"

The kid was worried how stupid his screaming would look in the video.

"This looks *great*," Ken said, fucking. He peered at the camera.

Tick, tick, tick . . .

The kid's dull, red butt getting slopped with some runny come. Splat, splat . . . splat.

Then the man sucked the kid's miniature cock till it shot a white drop at the roof of his mouth.

Ken stuck out his tongue, showing the camera his prize.

Tick, tick, tick . . .

After Robin came, he looked insanely at Ken.

*W*hen the telephone rings, Ziggy swipes it. The receiver's all . . . greasy. "Hello," he says, basically normal again, though he does have to swallow some wobbly snot right away.

"What's up?" asks Calhoun's deep, vibrant voice.

"Wow, Calhoun! You're awake. It's . . . late, right?"

"I guess." Calhoun chuckles.

"I'm just working on my magazine. What's going on with you?" Ziggy plops down on the sagging corner of his bed.

"Well, um . . . did my shot. Thinking a little. Not much. Oh, I watched that videotape."

"Yeah?" Ziggy waits, but there's just the warm, indefinable silence that radiates out of Calhoun between every sentence. It's always a drag not to be right there talking in person, but, Calhoun being Calhoun, meaning private, especially of late, Ziggy can't quite respond how he'd wish, and say something like 'I really miss you.' So . . . "And?" he asks.

"I don't know," Calhoun answers, and laughs. "Why exactly did you want me to see it?"

"For your take," says Ziggy. "'Cos I'm trying to figure out what I should think about it, and you're the person I most love and trust and all that. So . . . yeah, just your opinion." He immediately realizes he shouldn't have said the word *love,* and sort of snuggles the receiver into his ear, cheek, listening for subtle stuff.

"Hm. Well, you were into it, right? At the time?"

"Yeah, yeah. It's complicated. I was lonely, blah, blah, blah, you know? And my uncle's interesting in a way. You met him."

"Yup," says Calhoun. "Didn't much like the guy." He laughs. "Tries too hard. Or he did with me."

"That's 'cos he's, like, attracted to you."

"Yeah, well . . ." Calhoun breathes out, annoyed probably. "Whatever you want to do. But I thought the video was disgusting."

"Okay," Ziggy says, reassured. "I mean, I knew it was disgusting, but now I'm . . . sure. Thanks." There's a brief stretch of silence between them, which feels harsh to Ziggy, but, seeing as how Calhoun's much less talkative since he got into heroin, maybe it's just a kind of newfangled, natural space in the friendship. "So, uh . . . was it weird watching the video while on, like, heroin?"

"I don't know the difference anymore," says Calhoun. "You really should try shooting up sometime."

"Yeah." That seems to induce another uninterpretable silence.

"No, forget I said that." Calhoun chuckles. "What do you want me to say? The video bugged me. And I'm not gay, so I can't really form an opinion. I . . . I wish bullshit like that didn't happen, I guess."

"Me too," Ziggy says. "Definitely." He snorts kind of weakly. "Anyway, fuck it, uh . . . When do I get to hang out with you next?"

"Mm . . . I guess tomorrow's okay, if you want. But call before you come, in case I'm writing."

"Cool. Hey, yeah, how's your novel?"

"Oh . . . it's stalled, but . . . I've got some . . . mm, ideas."

"Well . . ." Shit. Ziggy clenches his jaw to keep from wondering aloud if Calhoun wouldn't write more without heroin. "I'll . . . call you, like, in the late morning?" he squeaks.

"Fine." Calhoun clears his throat. "See ya."

"Yeah, uh—"

Click.

Calhoun's mouth's hanging open. His thoughts, emotions, etc., are so indistinct it's like . . . what? . . . that they've splintered to . . . atoms somewhere in his overtaxed brain or . . . whatever. Every idea's uncooperative, mush. That's the point. Affection does this to him. And Ziggy's so beyond affectionate it's bewildering. Calhoun's only long-term reference point when it comes to emotion is Wendy, his mother, who tells him she loves him *all the time,* eyes haywire with alcoholic exuberance, though nothing much else that transpires between them is as simple as that supposedly ultimate sentiment. She's a total neurotic, which may make her love a lot spookier than Ziggy's, and, well, more understandable. Because of his screwed-up upbringing, Calhoun thinks human love is an outmoded concept. It does not compute, as they say, though he's learned to use "love" in his fiction when needed. That's different. If love's ever an issue outside art, like now via Ziggy, or sometimes with Josie, part of him gravitates to that supposed love very conventionally, and part of him's sort of appalled but can't exactly control the first part, except in terms of the way he responds, words-wise. He has theories galore about how well the world seems to function when one maintains distance from all other people. At some point in the past he'd been weak—a confused adolescent, obedient to parents and lazily Christian. Later, having read a little Nietzsche in school, he decided, among other things, that the world was preprogrammed by Satan or God or whoever, and, semibelieving this theory, as he continues to do on occasion, human beings are viruses. Thus, nothing matters. Self-absorption's the rule, if one follows that logic. But, at the same time, being stuck in the stupid real world, he can't help but realize he's an asshole for not just announcing, 'I love you too, Ziggy.' Because that's the truth, he supposes. Certainly he's grateful. Plus there's a great chance his gratitude constitutes love in itself. Didn't he read that somewhere? Calhoun looks at the phone, even reaches his hand out to call Ziggy back, but, seconds later, the logic behind that idea just . . . dissipates? And he zones out, mouth open, eyes glassy, hands splayed in his lap. Looks bad, but it feels unbelievable. Tick, tick, tick . . .

Dark blue air, starless, accompanied by crickets, bird chirps, and the occasional revving of cars whose ghostly headlights have somehow infiltrated the overgrown bushes and trees that parenthesize Ziggy's dad's house, throwing flashes, streaks, smears, general washes across a, oh . . . five-foot-square chunk of the backyard fence. Pretty. Ziggy hugs his knees, watches the lights, eyes essentially dry now. His hand's okay. His stupid feet aren't that thrashed after all. They could be bad pottery. They're practically scabbing already. The *New Day Rising* cassette's on its umpteenth play. He's trying to fantasize why he's upset into a single frame comic, but his emotions are too, uh, nearby now, too . . . focused? *I Apologize* No. 20 is already heavy on drawings where giant stick figures rape tiny stick figures. And that's all, blink, blink. Ziggy can, blink, blink, blink, picture right now . . . "Oh, fuck." His eyes fix on the phone. Fucking ring, he thinks. Tick, tick, tick . . . Okay, then *explode*, he rethinks, and adopts a, like, telekinetic or whatever stare. Tick, tick . . . *"Come on."* Tick . . . He grabs the thing, groaning a little. "Shit." Poke, poke, poke, poke . . .

Click.

"H-hello," Nicole mumbles. She's under that cloud again.

"Hi, I'm really sorry," Ziggy whispers into the mouthpiece. "It's me. I just had this idea that I'd come see you . . . now?"

"N-n-now? Okay, but . . ." She yawns. ". . . why?"

" 'Cos . . . I'm sort of . . . freaking out." Ziggy's lips silently form the word *please* about seventeen times in quick succession.

"Well, okay. I live at 7322 Vena Mondt Road. Do you know where that is? Near the corner of Kroening?"

Ziggy props the receiver between his shoulder and jaw, stands, pulling on the nearest clothes he can reach. "Yeah, I know where that is. But, uh . . . I have to . . . hitchhike, so . . . I may take . . . a while, but I'm leaving . . . this second." He squats down, feels around for socks, shoes.

"Ziggy, I . . . I'm trusting you. Shit. Look, when you get here, go through the gate—"

"Yeah, yeah. Wait, should I bring pot or whatever?" His mind does a search of the kitchen. "Or . . . beer?"

"No! Look, just . . . get here as soon as you can." There's a click as she hangs up.

"Yeah, great, bye." He drops the receiver into its

niche, zips up his jeans jacket. Then he crouches amid the ugly, multihued rubble of ex-furniture, ex-books, ex-posters, etc., for a second, loading his pockets with things he might need. Little black phone book, house key, Certs, lighter, Swiss Army knife, condoms, folded-up copy of *I Apologize* No. 19 . . .

*R*obin faked sleep, even drooling a little.

Ken made a phone call. Stroking the kid's butt, he hyped it to one of his customers.

Blah, blah, blah . . .

They were still in the "motel."

Robin secretly soaked in Ken's fucked-up affection.

"Hey," Ken said after a while, shook Robin.

"Yeah?" The kid yawned.

"Talk to this guy." Ken held the receiver above Robin's ear, mouth.

In the phone, someone breathed.

"Hello?" Robin asked.

"You made a video with Ken," said a voice with an out-of-town accent. "Tell me about yourself."

Robin yawned.

"I understand you're of Scandinavian descent. Are you blond?"

"My grandparents are British."

"Ken claims you're gorgeous."

"Yeah, he likes me." Robin grinned. He looked up at Ken, who was grinning too. But when their eyes met, all happiness faded out.

Ken took back the phone. "It'll be ready next weekend," he said, listened. "Okay, any requests? We're halfway through." And he listened again. "Easy. Pleasure."

The kid rolled over onto his back.

"Little dick, though," Ken said. "To be perfectly honest." A few seconds later he hung up.

Robin looked at Ken's fatness. "I don't know why, but you don't gross me out. No offense."

"You getting tired?" Ken asked.

"Yeah." Robin yawned. "But I can't fall asleep."

"These'll work." Ken slid open a drawer in the bedside table prop, seized a pill bottle. "Take three," he said, screwing the lid off.

Robin washed all three down with his lukewarm beer.

"Let's get a few hours' shut-eye," the man announced. "Then we'll finish up."

Robin rolled over onto his stomach. "Can you turn off those lights?"

"Yeah." Ken was studying the butt yet again. It looked totally different, more . . . squarish, more adult. "Don't you have parents who'll care where you are?"

"I'm out a lot," Robin slurred, a little drugs in his voice. "Seeing Slayer and shit."

Robin's butt was magnetic again. So Ken reached

over, spread its skimpy crack with his thumbs. He forced about an inch of one fingertip into the asshole.

"This feels weird," Robin mumbled.

Ken twisted the finger. "You're gorgeous," he said, sort of out of control for a second. Inside, the kid's butt was profound for some reason. Why? The temperature maybe?

Robin opened his eyes, as if he wanted to say something back, but instead he just lay there and blinked at Ken's mottled, white, jiggling thigh.

Ken probed.

So it must have been eight in the morning, New York time. I was sprawled across the bed, studying some gray air outside, for my apartment faced a narrow air well. Too horny to sleep, I did my best to think peacefulesque thoughts. Still, no matter how rural they grew, Ziggy, nude, formed the centerpiece of every image.

Eventually I gave in and shuffled the possible hardcore scenarios re: my young son, most of which were rewrites of his stories of Brice's "abuse," as Ziggy termed their odd sexual relationship. These true-to-life stories had always enticed me—I would literally ache post-recounting—yet, heretofore, they'd seemed crude, or too crudely relayed, to be inspirational.

I "saw" Ziggy punched, kicked, pummeled down to the floor, clothing ripped away—Brice was infused with unusual strength to, well, fuel this scenario—and there, *there* was my darling's firm, dusky white ass. (A guess.) Brice, a red-headed sketch with a very large penis, fucked Ziggy—fierce, violent strokes—that was his style in the old days at least—throwing punches, etc. When things became dangerously roughhouse, I broke down the door, shotgunned Brice, rescued Ziggy, and nursed his innumerable wounds. But nursing gradually devolved into the world's most elaborate rim job.

The deeper I rimmed, the more fluid my target became—simultaneously the spanking, if speculative image of Ziggy's asscheeks, and that of a second, more immediately available rump. It "belonged" to Osamu, a seventeen-and-a-half-year-old modern dance student who lived two floors below in my building. I'd been preparing this boy—without his knowledge, of course, though he was obviously nursing an innocent crush on me, that much was sure—for a roll in the sack ever since we met shopping for organic pears in the health food store just up our street.

So, half the time I "went to town" on my fantasy object, it was Osamu, not Ziggy, I ravaged, with no discernible shift—even slight, up or down—in enthusiasm, focus, or degree of emotional involvement, an equanimity I found rather curious, even amidst my temporary, desire-induced noncriticality.

The light was bright enough outside to call it a day. In the next several minutes, I devised a little scheme whereby my fall guy—for that's how Osamu appeared in light of my son's availability—would be allowed to compete unknowingly in an equitable contest with Ziggy. Then, refining the "hows" of this featherweight bout—more on that later—I masturbated halfheartedly until further notice.

*C*alhoun sits back, still relatively high, thank God, eating blueberry yoghurt. The taste tickles its almost bland way through the stinkier aftertaste of a half-pack of cigarettes. On his laptop computer screen: one paragraph of his novel-in-progress. The last sentence dangles before a pulsating cursor. It's an intricate beginning of a description of Gwen, a character based on his long-distance girl-friend. Like the novel itself, this description has reached a kind of comatose state for the moment. She, the novel, lie in an impenetrable stillness just outside his grasp. Oh, sometimes he'll go back and change a word, punctuation. But he's too pleasantly settled to do more than fiddle around with his accomplishments sort of admiringly. It's almost perfection how heroin nails other people and places generally at the distance he'd like them to halt. If only the drug wasn't so fucking expensive. There's the rub. To be happy, to hustle his parents for money to pay off his dealers, he has to concede a portion of his brain to the conventional world. Because, despite his philosophy, Calhoun's too sentimental and nervous to rip off the populus, much as he hates human beings in theory. And this politesse leaves him virtually jailed in his desk chair. Oh, sometimes he lies around on the bed that rests four feet away. On rarer occasions he wanders through his sweaty, windowless loft. With its half-finished drywalls and crooked corridors, it suggests a cheap carnival fun house. Surely he painted it that way on purpose, he can't quite remember. As a child, one had scared him so much the police had to come in and escort him out. No doubt it would seem cheesy as hell now. Sad, he supposes. Still, everything's equal, which is to say irrelevant, from the spectacular, fogged vantage point of wherever he is at the moment.

"Thanks for the lift, sir." Slam. Ziggy runs up Nicole's parents' driveway, knees slightly bowed, arms straight out, fingers splayed like a tightrope walker's, pockets rattling they're so packed with bullshit. The front yard's a small national park complete with hills, lake . . . "Jesus." The mansion's facade is an exact replica of the White House, at least in the dark. Behind a small fleet of parked luxury cars is a chain-link fence overgrown with clumpy dying or dead vines. As soon as he's un-latched that gate Nicole mentioned, and slipped through, a little square window with opaque, mottled glass, like in shower doors, illuminates way, way, way up near the roof. The fuzzy silhouette of a hand moves across it. Ziggy relatches the gate, then stands around in a kind of court-

yard looking idly at three tilted bicycles. Ten-speeds. Ital-
ian, he guesses. Eventually a door he can barely make out
to the left opens, revealing a wisp of Nicole. "Ziggy,
here," ushers her ashen voice. He squeezes inside the
house. Odor of . . . corn bread? She's dressed in a bathrobe
that looks like some grandma's fur coat, at first glance
anyway. Her dishwater blond hair's loose, tangled, hanging over her painfully smart eyes. Wishing he'd showered,
he trails her even-better-than-he'd-pictured ass through a
dark hall, up steep, darker-yet stairs, sneaking occasional
sniffs of his armpits. P.U., he thinks, fanning the immediate air. Right turn, down another hall lined with rotten
paintings of . . . whatever, villas, and they're inside . . .
well, Nicole's room presumably. It's so brightly lit, he has
to cup his eyes. "Stay here," she whispers, reentering the
hall. As soon as her footsteps have faded away, he spits
twice in one palm, shoves it under the band of his underwear, and cleans his grubby cock, studying the room's
furnishings, which are too . . . organized or whatever. His
eye catches a sparkling mirror hung over her, uh, antique
dresser. He moves close, squints at his reflection until it's
in focus, then revolves like a beauty pageant contestant,
evaluating his details, one eye on the doorway. Cute,
yeah, okay, he decides. At least in clothes. Nicole's stuck
a few Polaroids here and there in the mirror's frame with
. . . Bart Simpson refrigerator magnets? Ugh. Some smiling, remotely familiar jock hugs her in most of the
pictures.

Creak.

Ziggy turns, startled. "Uh, yeah?"

"Hi." She's clicking the door shut behind her. "Those are pictures of Jim," she says, and tiptoes over to Ziggy. "I used to love him. Then I figured out he was a fascist from talking to my psychiatrist. And Jim is one, I know, but now I miss him again so I put these back up. You'd hate him."

Ziggy nods hurriedly. " 'Cos of his politics?"

"That. And for how he treats me. You, well, mm . . ." Her hazel eyes sort of sizzle his, like they're car headlights and his burnt-out sockets are tunnels. "People don't matter that much to artistic types," she continues, a very slight warp in her lips. "I mean as individuals. So they don't treat girls differently than they treat boys, which is cool. I tend to be interested in artistic types because I'm an artist."

"Really?" Ziggy asks, feeling relatively lost. Her beauty—specifically those blinding eyeballs, turned-up nose, and shadowed lips, not to mention that hair—is sort of erasing his senses a little. Uncle Ken had just explained the other day how that happens with beauty. "Well, there are definitely people I like and don't like," he admits.

"What about with people you fuck?" She's looking off at the Polaroids or their reflection or all three. "Do you miss them afterwards? Or do you wish you never fucked them? Or . . ." She squints. ". . . neither?"

"Yeah, yeah, I know what you mean, uh . . ." Ziggy scrunches his face up, trying to mentally rewatch TV shows where scenes like this one occur. "See, I have all

these reasons for doing things, uh . . . Can we sit down?"
He lurches toward the bed, but she knows a little short-
cut, beats him there, cannonballing some stuffed bears,
sock monkeys, Raggedy Andys, etc., crowded up against
a vast if haphazardly carved, uh . . . Indonesian-style
headboard? Ziggy stops at the foot of the bed, tensed,
pondering his options, then sits cross-legged on the neatly
folded blue comforter. "There, okay," he continues, settling. "Uh, that's a hard question." He glances at her, but
his eyes keep getting snagged by stuffed animals' stares.
"I'm sort of bisexual so far. When I do it with guys—not
that I have very much—it's, well . . . love, I guess.
Uh . . ." All the toys' fake attention is weirding him out,
so he checks his lap, legs. "And, uh, I have to be positive
with guys that I don't get emotional, 'cos I'm so . . . I hate
words like this, but the school therapist tells me I'm
'needy,' okay?" He tries Nicole's face again. She looks
. . . a little *too* interested maybe. "With girls, though, it's
just . . . I don't know . . . fun? So guys and girls are, like,
different situations, and I don't know which I like better
yet."

Nicole frowns like she understands his dilemma.

"Hey, did you ever know this guy Calhoun?" he
adds. "I mentioned him before. He was a senior last
year?"

She squints. "Maybe." Her squint gets more
wrinkly. "Didn't he turn into a junkie?"

"Yeah, exactly. Well, in a perfect world, he and I
would be boyfriends. 'Cos I like him more than any-

body—we're best friends, right?—and, you know, he likes me tremendously too, I *think*. But, anyway, he's even straighter than me, so . . . so . . ." And Ziggy makes a squishy noise with his mouth. "But then again . . ." He grins really forcibly. ". . . probably what makes us so close is that we don't sleep together. And, you know, it's great the way it is now. And I'm probably not gay either, like I said. It's like we're brothers, I guess. *I* don't know." He shrugs. *"So . . ."* Ziggy looks at his thumb, which he raises slightly and turns like it's a diamond that's caught the light, trying to make his eyes look bedazzled. "That's my story. What's your thinking about sexual stuff?"

"Mm." Nicole rolls over onto her back, squints at the ceiling. Ziggy recalls noticing a mobile up there, but he refuses to seem imitative and check, though it's hard to keep pretending his thumb's interesting. After ten, fifteen seconds, she grins at whatever's up there or in her mind, and says—whispers, actually—"It's fun." Ziggy's still pretend-studying his thumb, deconstructing her answer, when, whoosh, she bursts out of the stuffed animal heap and flops down on her stomach, squeak, squeak, very near his left kneecap, eyeing him from below, uh, well, erotically, he's almost sure. "Maybe we should . . . sleep," she adds. Nicole folds her hands, bounces them two or three times off her puffy lips. "I don't know how else to say it."

Ziggy grins insanely. "No, no, no, that'd be great." His facial skin's so taut it probably looks like those nylon stocking masks people wear when they try to rob banks. Luckily Nicole has risen up on her haunches, unknotting

the belt of her robe. "So I'll . . . uh, undress too, I guess."
He cocks an eyebrow, like, roguishly?

"Mm," she says, fiddling.

"So, uh, okay. Cool." Ziggy slides off the bed,
winces, hunched up, a mildly deformed mannequin with
body odor from hell, fingers stuck to his Hüsker Dü
T-shirt. "Come on, man," he mumbles, not loud enough
for her to hear. He throws off his jacket, whips the T-shirt
up over his head, P.U., unsnaps, yanks down the rest of
his outfit, then sits sort of demurely on bed's edge, realizing his feet smell like Indian food. Keep armpits shut, he
thinks. What else . . . ? Behind him she's already naked,
lying crookedly across the bed like a thick spill of something that's so comfortable it's just waiting to evaporate.
Shit. Ziggy turns away, looks forlornly at the out-of-focus
door, contemplating escape, elbows dug into his knees,
chin in palms, positive he's too skinny. He can't not imagine a spine, ribs, etc., rising garishly from the pimpled
flesh of his back like . . . whatever, the Loch Ness monster,
and, three feet behind him, Nicole's eyes—no, her whole
perfect face—studying that stretch of his anatomy with a
look of, uh . . . horror?

But when he bites his lip, turns around, she's still as
calm as a spill, eyes far, far away but not angry, reflecting
the color if not the actual, physical look of the mobile,
whose dozens of dangling white pieces—Ziggy takes a
quick peek—are obviously supposed to make one think of
a drifting cloud bank.

Ziggy scoots toward Nicole, first a couple of inches.

Deep breath. Then he splays one damp hand on the blanket, leans sideways, makes absolutely sure her eyes are warm. Yeah. Raising up on his knees, Ziggy crawls over, straddles her, flops. Nicole's breasts sort of flatten between their rib cages, which looks terrifying, like they're about to, uh, rupture, but feels . . . transcendental? Like every girl Ziggy's had sex with, she hugs him, maybe a little too limply in this case. Still, he starts kissing her face, neck, licks a zigzaggy trail to those breasts, which have really bounced back, sort of slurping their nipples for several minutes at least, blissed out. Nicole's smell, especially here for some reason, is so fucking faint, unlike his own body's pointless pollution. It's more, like, uh . . . flowers, as boring as that idea is, mixed with something less obvious. . . . With his favorite meal maybe, whatever *that* is. Probably some Mexican item. Burritos? Is that too . . . insulting? Ouch, says Nicole's voice. "What?" A hand slides beneath his face, lifting it off the breasts. Must be his chin stubble, such as it is. "Sorry," he whispers, and peers at her crumpled visage. It nods, crumpling even more. Then Ziggy licks cautiously, on tongue tip, toward her lips, which are so much more open than his that his pucker falls way down inside like a little bucket. Ouch. He sips some fizzy saliva, face all steamed by her breath, if that's possible. Puff, puff, puff . . . Most girls he's fucked have unraveled their hugs about this point in time to mean, Lick farther down, give me head—that's a guess—but, if anything, Nicole's hug's grown . . . artistic or something, like her fingers are spelling out words on his shoulders and back. If so, they're in some other language. Anyway, she's okay. "Nicole?" he asks croakily, raising up. Her throat makes a whirring noise. "Can I fuck you? Uh . . . sorry to be so . . ." Same whirring noise, but centered more in her mouth. "Thanks," he squeaks. "Be right back." Ziggy pries himself loose, scrambles off the bed, digs around inside his jeans jacket pocket, comes up with a condom, pops it free of its silvery package, and lassoes his cock, which is intensely hard, thank God. Unrolling the condom, Ziggy slides back on top of Nicole, who not only hugs him again, but sort of crushes her face against his. "Okay," he mumbles, pinching his shrink-wrapped hard-on between a thumb and forefinger. He stabs it around in her pubic hair. Thud, thud . . . "Oh, shit." It sinks into the ragged, soaked . . . bull's-eye? "Sorry." Wow, *unbelievable*. His body's spontaneously combusting or whatever. "Shi-i-i-it, Nicole." He rears back, looks down into her eyes, which are foggy slices, panting, bucking his hips. "Yes, yes, ye-e-e-ess . . ." Ziggy comes. His vision bleaches. He's collapsing on top of her, arms straight out, sort of like a malfunctioning plane on a do-it-yourself landing strip. His ass knots, unknots for about half a minute. Nicole's sort of gone into pillow mode, letting whatever happens happen, seemingly cool about everything. Ziggy's condom—cock too, naturally— starts shriveling up in her cunt. It flops out, getting goo, etc., on them both, but especially her, thanks to gravity. His face is smashed all to shit on her throat, which she's clearing occasionally. One of those grumbles is particularly loud. That's when he realizes she's not hugging him anymore. Shit. Nicole's arms departed his torso somewhere down the line. He's just sort of sprawled on her body like someone protecting someone else from an imminent explosion. So he peels himself off, causing this subtle rip sound, and drops onto his side, almost matching her crumply pose about two or so feet to the left. He can't look back, so he fastens his eyes to the lame-o mobile overhead. But it holds so little interest he can't help spacing out into somewhere where everything—Nicole included—is just another cloud or not even around or whatever.

It's weird, he decides after a second, how the girl experience is almost, like, oppositional to the man experience, at least based on going to bed with Brice, with Uncle Ken that one time, and from watching porn videos, plus gay scenes in novels he's skimmed, uh . . . And sort of how passionate he feels about Calhoun, if that counts. Whereas with Nicole, make that with every girl so far, sex ends up being so . . . planned in advance, not by him obviously, but by history or whatever. So no matter how wild sex gets, he's still following this preset, like, outline, point by point, and when an experience is over, such as now with Nicole, it sort of gradually dilutes into a zillion other people's identical experiences, until Ziggy feels . . . used in a way? Or maybe it's just his rebelliousness problem. Still, gay sex seems to have this great scariness quotient, whereby no two situations are ever alike, as far as he can tell. So even though Ziggy feels basically the same about girls pre– and post–getting laid, as opposed to a lot more or less deep emotion for guys, he thinks he may end up straight, period, assuming he has a choice. Remember, *remember*, he thinks, to compare this Nicole experience to whatever Roger does to his body, uh . . . day after tomorrow? No, shit, *tomorrow*. "Uh, Nicole, what time is it?" he asks, peering cautiously in her direction.

"Almost showering time." She turns her head, studies his crotch. "For me at least." Those mind-boggling eyes burst into his stupid orbs for a second.

"Oh, uh, ha ha ha." Ziggy immediately feels stiff head to toe, like a corpse might if it was alive or just mentally aware or whatever. "So, that was nice."

"Yeah." She looks away, which makes it seem like she doesn't in fact mean she enjoyed it. "But . . ." And she squints at something over his shoulder. ". . . do you always have sex fast like that?"

"No, why?" he asks. Her face looks the least friendly he's ever seen it. "Oh, God, I'm sorry. I'm nervous, I guess. Don't take it personally. You're great, you're beautiful. I'm just . . . weird."

"Well . . . it was sort of . . . hyper," she says distractedly. Maybe she's spotted the mirror, uh, yeah, and is comparing their sex to her experiences with Jim, because her face looks uncertain now, or, like . . . respectful, but, overall, just too attractive to gauge. "And . . . you're kind of hyper in general," she continues after a few moments. "So I should have known. But now I wish that we'd waited, or that I'd waited anyway." She smiles at

. . . the mirror again? "Or that you'd brought along some pot after all."

"Yeah, pot would've helped," Ziggy says. "It really does in situations like this, yeah, yeah, 'cos I'm so sped up. If I get too stoned, you know, it's hard in another way though, ha ha. With guys it isn't that big a deal because they always find something to do with me, no matter what, but with girls there's this weird line you have to, like, walk between fucked up and sober, and I don't walk it very well, I guess."

"It's not that," she says. "I was just ready for it to take longer." Then she refocuses on him, still smiling. *Weird*. "That's a compliment, Ziggy."

I was watching Osamu spear, transfer forkfuls of scrambled eggs from the plate to his mouth, chew, then swallow, his shiny cheeks flexing and rippling in nervous bunches. When he noticed the strange intensity of my gaze, he'd halt midchew and squint, at which points I'd shake myself out of some rapturous daydream and smile amiably, which reassured my young guest, or so it appeared, since he would fixate on chewing again.

Osamu's head was a grayish brown oval, with narrow, murky eyes that seemed three-quarters surface yet bottomless. Wee nose. Fat, purple lips. Squarish ears bracketed by a virtual haystack of black hair that flip-flopped along with his gesticulations. His voice, while pitched high and even squeaky at times, had already attained a mannered evenness of phrasing that spoke of adultlike aplomb, creating the illusion that one could converse with him satisfactorily on any subject. Still, the strain of having to appear knowledgeable about certain topics wore away at his composure at times; he would sulk or seem distracted, while I reverted to a soothing, fatherly condescension.

Osamu had just cleaned his plate when I began to explain my dilemma. Speaking to teenagers, especially when I was bent on seduction, could be arduous, as I was required to convey my desire—a desire I couldn't possibly expect teens to fathom—while downgrading my vocabulary to meet teens' semideveloped mentalities partway. This was definitely a problem regarding Osamu, since he had the spacy demeanor endemic to dancers. So, as I outlined my impending trip West, and how it might include sex with a certain exquisite young someone, I made clear to Osamu, in relatively straightforward sentences, that if I found this someone as enticing postsex as I did at that moment, it might mean never seeing my young guest again, for certain complicated-to-explain reasons. But perhaps, I said, if Osamu could offer a sexual encounter himself, say right then, I might reevaluate our future together.

Osamu listened, trying to hide his more than obvious distress. When I paused for a moment, he voiced this confusion, and I offered comfort, in theory at least, by comparing the formal structure and properties of the sex act to dancing. That made him laugh, which I considered a small victory. Then I queried him until we'd boiled his concern down to terror of contracting AIDS, in light of which I reassured him my test came back negative, cajoled, changed the subject, etc., and, in no time at all, he'd agreed to this "project."

As I'd expected, Osamu's nude body was perfectly formed, as unpored as tinted cellophane, at least from a few feet away—sleek, shimmering, and packed full of neatly shaped, well-hidden bones and eye-tickling musculature, the latter made more garish still by the nervous, balletic-style poses he struck while he stripped. Something had already stiffened his rather too purplish prick, which, not so surprisingly, encouraged yours truly to nod toward the bed.

*C*alhoun's squatting in front of a toilet, the bowl and rim marbled with urine drops, most dried to scabs, some embedded with pubic hairs. The entirety's unfocused, a skinny oval of . . . threatening clouds. Or maybe it's . . . almost . . . an old-fashioned frame around his distorted reflection—elongated face and throat blurred with pale vomit. He's empty. His stomach's still scrunching up every few seconds. Groans, etc., boom through the room, loud as breaks in the sound barrier. They're weirdly comforting, as are the twists in the skin of his waist where those megataxed insides freak out in their mysterious ways. His face is the ugliest it's ever been, not just because of the gross-smelling mirror. Partially it's the angle. But mostly it's how uncontrolled he looks now. His features are so narrow and grayish they could be an ax blade, a few chunks knocked out here and there. That's the opposite of how he wants them to read, whatever that opposite is. Maybe angelic, but masculine too, not a fashion model's exactly, not fake. It's just that people should wonder what's in here, mentally he means. If Ziggy's right he's a genius of some sort. That's thinking too loftily, of course. Or is it? Is he really up there with Rimbaud, as some teachers once hinted? Is Ziggy's huge admiration a preview of what's way out there in the future? Calhoun rocks back on his heels, blinking ferociously at the raised toilet lid, in which he doesn't reflect in the slightest. "Hm." By now the nausea's waning. He eases up to his feet, struggling ten or so steps to the right, and looks into his bathroom's real mirror, balancing his hands on the basin's raised, filthy white border. His unkempt blond hair, trumpet ears, fine lips, big nose, startled greenish blue eyes are composed, even now, although he's technically drugged out and worthless to anyone else, he supposes. So . . . whatever whoever decides or can't decide about him is extraneous. That's excellent news, if . . . depressing too. "Hm." Depressing . . . how? Okay, let's eliminate Ziggy's opinion. He's obviously in love, which undermines his assessment. Done. Fine. Who cares? All alone in the world, Calhoun pushes his worn-out face close to the mirror and tells himself, "No one appreciates you," then smiles as sympathetically as possible. But, at least in reflection, it looks like a grimace.

*W*hile Nicole showers, Ziggy hurls on B.O.-scented clothes, touring her belongings, most of which seem too nondescript and conventionally trendy for someone so sharp. Still, Ziggy's used to how wealthier people surround themselves with stuff that's sort of simplistic or dull on the eyes, ears, nose, etc. In her case, miniature porcelain animals, beige stationery, Michael Jackson CDs, chalky colored, artsy framed posters for sixties jazz festivals, a hanging air freshener disguised as a biomorphic sculpture . . . It's like, Hey, world, I'm rich, leave me fucking alone! Or something. He cringes, trying to enter her brain, but the room stays off-putting. Eventually she's back, drippy, robed. He uncreases the copy of *I Apologize* No. 19. There's a terrible drawing of Jeffrey Dahmer raping, etc., Konerak Sinthasomphone on the cover. "Read this when I'm not around," Ziggy says, shoves it at her. She eyeballs the front, back, lays it not that carefully on a pile of *Sassy*s on her dresser. Then Ziggy stands around watching her dress, which makes him hard again. They sneak downstairs, chug-a-lug Cheerios and grape juice. She pets their family's sheepdog, Anastasia, which makes Ziggy sad for some reason. The British housekeeper with frizzy, gray hair—Millicent someone—drives them to school, not seeming to care about Ziggy's having obviously stayed overnight. Nicole's gotten more and more friendly postshower, so Ziggy stops torturing himself about fucking up with her sexually. She's almost girlfriendlike now in some weird way he can't figure out. They even sort of dry-hump through their clothes in the Mercedes's backseat, while Millicent hums the melody of . . . "The Impossible Dream"? He lets himself trust Nicole's affection for ten minutes, tops. "Bye, Millicent, thanks," etc. Now they stand and kiss again by the faculty parking lot. Ziggy's so comfortable and, well, happy his eyes keep rolling back in his head involuntarily. But . . . Rrrring. School itself might as well be a giant ice sculpture, he feels so different, so . . . stiff and uncomfortable, yeah, the very second they pass through its ornate iron gate. Nicole waves, barreling off to some class, and Ziggy pretends to be strolling toward . . . whatever, Algebra I? He even deigns to shout, "Hi," at a couple of assholes he knows. When the crowds thin, he leans way back into a shadowy nook between two banks of book lockers, waiting, bored as shit, singing Hüsker Dü's "I Apologize" to himself, for the 8:15 bell. Rrrring. All clear. It's utterly quiet now. Cool. So he scoots down the hall, turns right, and quickly crosses the open-air quad, dead grass crunching under his stinky Adidas, into some older, more dilapidated school buildings. Tromp, tromp . . . Reaching the door, 17, that Annie's, ha ha, imprisoned behind, he turns the knob unbelievably slowly, pulls, reveals a cropped vista of the classroom itself. Typical. Top half becalmed by a dozen huge, bannerlike maps of the earth. Bottom half, a relative sprawl—decoration-clogged bulletin boards bracketing a messy regiment of desks, each one crammed with the blandly dressed figure of . . . whatever . . . some seventeen-year-old? Annie's a punky eyesore in the back row, staring haphazardly at something above Ziggy's head. Her wide, squarish face hangs open babyishly, forearms raised boxer-style, drumming to within an inch or two of the desktop. A quick, precise . . . Speed Metal rhythm, he guesses, knowing her tastes. Ziggy stares really intently at Annie's oblivious features, ear especially, and thinks, I need some drugs, repeating that sentence over and over until, sort of paranormally, her short, dyed black hair jiggles. Encouraged, Ziggy waves his hand close to his chest. Annie, seeming a bit more, like, human now, shifts her dilated eyes' focus to his subtle motion, and grins . . . wickedly? Ziggy gestures to come. Nodding, Annie faces front, shoots one arm into the map-colored upper atmosphere, such that her T-shirt sleeve falls, crumples up in the armpit, exposing a giant red mole . . . no, a Satan tattoo. Cool. A male, impatient, authoritarian voice asks her something—hard to hear what—then . . . "Diarrhea," Annie yells in that thick southern accent which makes her customers, Ziggy included, think she's so sweet and sexy. Students' uncontrolled laughter. "Thanks, y'all." She rockets to her feet, and hobbles directly at Ziggy, cross-eyed with mock nausea, one hand scrunching the waist of her holey black T-shirt.

* * *

"Quick, mah dude." Annie's originally from Alabama or somewhere. They streak down a deserted hall, past the garish, flaking Famous Scientists Then and Now mural, where Einstein's got his arm around . . . Jonas Salk's shoulders, if Ziggy remembers right, and into the former faculty john turned graffiti museum/drug-dealing den. "This here's what's available," the girl continues, pulling three Baggies out of her jeans pocket. "Oh, *hey,*" she says, pausing before what's still around of a mirror. "Ah love your magazine." She's checking the state of her hair in the mirror's dull, fractured surface. "Did ah tell you? Ah rilly, *rilly* relate to it." Satisfied or something, she goes over, lines up the little bags across the top of what used to be a pocket comb dispenser. "Pot, coke . . . ," she says.

"What's that?" Ziggy asks, indicating the off-white, clogged powder in one.

"Heroin," Annie says, sort of beaming. "Mah new, um . . . what do they call it? You know, when stores have a . . . mah new *lahn?*"

Ziggy nods like he gets it. "Well," he says. "I need to get through a sex scene I might not, like, know how to be part of exactly. Any recommendations?"

Her big, clownlike lips wrench apart, the lower one wobbling about an inch from the upper, two nicotine-stained front teeth sparkling dimly between. After a bit, the lips pinch back together, lengthen into an uncertain grin, and Annie slurps down some excess saliva, it sounds like. "What kahnd of sex would be hard to git through, mah dude?" She cackles, dropping heavily onto a former toilet.

"I'm sure I told you about my two dads, and how one is this rock critic who lives in New York? He's, like, uh . . . I sort of want to sleep with him."

"Dude," she whispers. "But . . . he gives you an allowance, raht? That's what it's about, *raht?*"

Ziggy shrugs, mumbles, "Not really."

Annie frowns, leaps up, runs over and studies her row of products. "As a businesswoman, and not as a person who lahks you a lot, ah'd say . . ." She squints/frowns at Ziggy. "First, is havin' your orgasm part of the plan?"

Ziggy reruns a typical fantasy where he's being rimmed, fucked, etc., by Roger, then mentally rescans his dad's pornolike letter. "I . . . guess not."

Annie holds out the bag with the off-white powder. "Heroin," she says. "And not jus' 'cos ah got a whole lotta the stuff on mah hands."

"Are you sure?" Ziggy's thinking of Calhoun, obviously, not to mention how scary old what's-his-name . . . Keith Richards looks in recent videos compared to how he looked on the Rolling Stones LPs in Brice's cobwebbed collection.

"Definitely," Annie says. "'Cos it gits you loose, raht?" She looks up at the bathroom's grungy ceiling, for inspiration maybe. Somebody's drawn a kind of technically accomplished red-and-black felt-tip chandelier that must appear semireal when you're loaded. "Most people git horny on heroin. Everybody gits less uptaht than usual. You can git hard, but, lahk ah said, people say you can't come." Then she blushes or something resembling a blush. "And you have those pretty green ahs, so you should realahze you'll look major drugged out. Your dad'll know you're on *somethin'*. And you may throw up raht after you snort it, but then you'll be fahn."

Ziggy's been nodding along, imagining himself stumbling all over the place. "So I should snort it *before* he comes over?"

She hands him the Baggie. "Or raht before you're gonna go to bed," she advises, pocketing the unpurchased products. "Tell your dad you wanna shower, raht? Lock yourself in the bathroom, snort that, give yourself fifteen minutes to barf and feel better, maybe longer, then use some Listerine and . . . *git down*."

"Thanks," Ziggy says, flipping the heroin Baggie from hand to hand. "But, so, it won't, like, give me diarrhea, will it?"

Annie's mouth flies wide open again for a second. "Only if you're accidentally allergic to it or somethin'." She's on her feet, stretching, anxious to split.

"And I . . . do it like . . . coke?" Ziggy holds out a twenty-dollar bill, figuring that should, well, cover it, hopefully. "'Cos a friend of mine shoots it. Calhoun. Do you know him?"

"Sure do."

"He's the greatest person who ever lived," Ziggy says, fiddling with the Baggie.

"Nahce gah." Annie smiles.

"And he's my *best friend.*"

Annie's just smiling, less impatiently maybe.

" 'Cos he shoots it, and, uh . . . I'm kind of concerned about him."

"Ah understand," she mumbles. "Well, snortin' it's easier on the system." She takes a few reverse baby steps, basically toward the door. "Look, don't worry, you'll be fahn." One arm rockets out, grabs the bill, folds, pockets it. A couple more steps. "But . . . listen, about Calhoun?" Annie frowns, checks her watch. "She-e-it," she says, heaving out some breath. And her head tilts way back. She sort of scrubs the "chandelier" with her eyes. They're watery. Either that or the reflection's intense. "Well, jus' keep on lovin' him, raht? 'Cos he deserves it, raht?" Now her eyes, which are definitely wet, yeah, meet Ziggy's, scrub a little, then jolt up to the ceiling again.

"Yeah, uh . . . thanks." Ziggy nods furiously.

Ken held up a two-foot rope of dyed blond human hair.

Robin lazed on his back. Head shaved, face pink from where Ken had used a washrag to scrub away Glam Metal makeup.

In the background, Slayer's LP was there again full blast.

"I took the liberty," Ken yelled.

Robin seemed like he half- to two-thirds understood.

Shaking the hair rope, Ken added, "'Cos . . . why fucking not?"

"I said *okay*," Robin slurred, about the head shaving.

Ken walked over, eased down. Tipping Robin onto his side, Ken twisted the bundle of hairs once, twice, three times, whipped it jump rope style over the kid's spaced-out head, and made a gag, quickly tying a knot.

Slayer: *Observing trance awaking state / Lying still unknowing / Reciting the passages of time / Prepare for the impaling.*

"Oh *yeah*." Ken laughed, sitting back.

Robin said something. Nobody heard what.

"I'm gonna switch on the camera," Ken yelled. He eased Robin onto his back. "Stay limp," he added. "Let me direct it."

Robin lay there.

"I like you," shouted Ken from the video camera. "You should hang out. You'd like my nephew. He's insane."

"Fuck off," said the kid through his hair gag.

The man shut one eye, zoomed in . . . in . . . in . . . An enlarging dime nipple.

"God, you're gorgeous." Ken sighed, very moved, awestruck, proud, etc.

*B*ending over to sip from a mossy water fountain, Ziggy hears a familiar voice, female, yeah, hopelessly en-

twined with . . . another girl's voice? They're chanting his
name out of sync, which sort of thrills him at first, like
he's a band being begged for an encore. Then, imagining
passersby's sneers, he gets totally paranoid. "Yeah?"
Ziggy straightens up, wiping some dew from his mouth,
chin. Nicole's walking his way down the hall with Cricket,
i.e., Andrew French, a chubby boy with long, straight
brown hair who always dresses in slightly outdated girls'
clothing. Ziggy's been strangely turned on by the oddball
of late, he has to admit, as insane as that sounds. So he
accompanies the pair for a few minutes, down one hall, up
another, trying to impress them both with the sorry details of his sexual abuse, which isn't that difficult a task,
it seems. Attractiveness, bizarre. It makes things so easy
at times, meaning now, since Cricket giggles continuously
the whole fucking way, like he/she thinks he/she's walking
along with Bill Murray or whoever. From the new, sneaky
way the transvestite eyes him when he's supposedly not
looking, ha ha, Nicole must've passed on the, uh, news
about their orgy last night, which is a little unnerving,
considering how clumsy, etc., he was, but . . . Thank God
there's their classroom door.

   "Go on," Nicole says, nudging Cricket. Students are
brushing by. "Ask him," she adds, and when Cricket just
looks away, grimacing, Nicole snorts and says, "Cricket
wants your cock, Ziggy. Okay, Cricket, give him your
number. God, you guys!"

   Still averting his/her eyes, Cricket, who, with his/
her pale, blocky face, looks Norwegian or something,
holds out a folded-up paper, then, cheeks instantaneously

empurpled, yuck, turns and dog-paddles into the class-room. "Bye," he/she mumbles.

"Talk to you later, Ziggy?" says Nicole, splitting. She looks over one shoulder, eyes wide and brows wiggling.

"Oh, uh . . . definitely," Ziggy shouts, walking away. He unfolds the note. Over Cricket's phone number—affected, curlicue handwriting, yuck—he/she's scrawled, *Maybe Saturday night?* That halts Ziggy mid-hall. If Cricket means his/her place, maybe Roger will play chauffeur, or, if Cricket intends to come over to Ziggy's house, Roger can go for a long walk, or . . . watch them fuck, or . . . join in? Ziggy finger-combs his dirty hair, scheming. The hall's emptied out. Several doors up on the left is his therapist's office. Dr. Michelle Carr. Oh yeah, Ziggy thinks, maybe . . . she'll . . . have some . . . advice . . . Rrrring. Or . . . Ziggy blinks . . . on the other hand . . . Blink, blink. He whips around, rips down the hall, taking a gentle right through the ornate iron gate, then a harder left into the public phone booth at the edge of the faculty parking lot.

Click.

"Mm-hm?" Lots of nightmarish breathing. Distorted Heavy Metal in the background. They really do sound incredible mixed together, if, yeah, okay, sort of corny.

"Uncle Ken?" Ziggy asks, catching his own breath. "What's going on?"

"A fair amount. But you're going to have to yell. Where're you calling from?"

"School!" Ziggy glances around. Nobody anywhere. "I'm about to leave! Can I come by for a while?" He silently mouths "please" a few times.

"Okay," Ken says after a moment of music. "But there's the same little problem as last night."

Ziggy mentally rewinds the morning, previous night, until he reaches their last conversation. "Oh, the Heavy Metal kid! He's still there?"

Either Ken laughs or something weird happens to and/or within the background music. Maybe one of those back-masked Satanic insertions that tell you to kill yourself.

"If you mean what you're doing with the Metal kid, that doesn't bother me!" Ziggy checks for bystanders again. Nope. Just a dirty, water-stained herd of inexpensive, samey-looking, mostly blue foreign cars. "But . . . will there be time to blab? I sort of need to!"

Same laughlike or Satanic noise. Then Ken obviously covers the mouthpiece with his hand, 'cos the music's squashed down to a shortwave radio–style hiss for a second or two. "Hey, come or don't," he announces upon his return. "I've got to go."

"I'm on my way. Bye." Ziggy's hanging up, eyes on the street, when he hears Uncle Ken, or maybe Satan, ha ha, bellow something, and hauls the receiver back to his right ear, mouth. "Did you yell?"

"Yeah. A possible alternate plan." Either the music

in the background is over or else it's just between songs. In any case, Ken's voice sounds a million times more . . . entertaining, complex . . . *something*. "Why don't you bring along that Calhoun kid?"

"Why?" Ziggy tenses.

"Bring Calhoun. We'll all get high. I'll talk to Robin here. Maybe we'll shoot a little something with Calhoun and him." The next song blasts on, covering Ken's voice and breathing, an aural avalanche of snarly, sort of melodic feedback.

Ziggy's shoulders and arms have seized up, making the receiver shake delicately in his hand. "Uh, isn't Calhoun sort of too old for you? Besides, he's, like, straight."

"You mean repressed." Ken snickers over the music. "Like you."

"Ha ha. Uh, not really! He's just, uh . . . *I* don't know! Anyway, he's my best friend, so, you know . . . forget it!" Ziggy slugs the phone. Again, again.

Ken breathes furiously a few times, which, mixed in with the Metal, is so . . . frightening or whatever, it makes Ziggy feel like his skin, veins, muscles, and stuff have gotten bunched around his skeleton, sort of like pajamas do after a bad night, but more . . . insidious. "Fine!" Ken's voice shouts. "Then . . . come over by yourself! Jesus . . . fucking—"

Click.

Click.

"Hello?" Calhoun's voice sounds . . . abrupt, like

he's annoyed someone's called. But it's obviously insane to second-guess someone so, like, amazing.

"It's me." Ziggy whispers for some reason. "So guess what? I got some heroin."

"Really? From where? Is it in tar form, or—"

"Yellow powder." Ziggy shoves the receiver between his shoulder and jaw, then pulls out the Baggie, cradling it secretively in one palm. "Or . . . off-white, I guess."

"Awesome!"

"Yeah, cool, huh?" Ziggy blurts, dancing on his toes a little.

"Hm . . ." Calhoun's voice trails for a second. "Maybe you shouldn't do it. I've been thinking about this. See, I'm constitutionally suited to opiates. But I don't know about you. And I'm thinking of quitting myself. And I don't want people blaming me if you pick up a habit."

"They won't." Ziggy's sort of confused. He rethinks his answer, left hand fingering some shallow wrinkles in his forehead. "I mean, I won't get a habit."

"You don't want this." Calhoun chuckles. "It's expensive for one thing."

Ziggy doesn't know how to phrase this, but . . . "Are you okay?"

"Yeah, I'm fine. But it'd be stupid for you to start when I'm thinking of quitting."

"No, I know. Actually, don't get pissed, but I wish you *would* quit, 'cos I keep worrying you're gonna O.D., and—"

"I won't," Calhoun mumbles.

"Are you . . . *sure,* 'cos . . ." Ziggy strums his forehead kind of punkily.

"Yeah, I'm sure!" Then Calhoun shuts up, but his silence is somehow more like whatever the opposite of silence would be. Like a scream? "Look, just . . . just don't do it."

"Okay, I won't." Ziggy's right hand crumples the Baggie.

"Hey, do whatever you want, though. Don't not do anything on my account."

"I don't *want* to." Ziggy reduces the Baggie to a wad in his fist.

Calhoun's voice squeaks frustratedly.

"I just . . . don't want to hurt you, you know? You're my best friend."

"Yeah," says Calhoun, either resigned or uncomfortably pleased or . . . something. Then, luckily, he chuckles.

"And I love you a lot. Sorry." Ziggy punches his forehead. That flattens the wrinkles out.

"Yeah, I know, I know. Just . . . do whatever you want."

"I *won't* do it."

"O-*kay!*"

"And I'll, uh . . . come over and see you . . . tomorrow," Ziggy adds as casually as he can.

"Yeah?" More silence or . . . turbulence. "When?"

"Uh, wait . . . oh, *shit.*" Ziggy pounds his forehead.

"My fucking *dad's* flying in from New York tomorrow, and I think we're going to, uh, sleep together, ha ha ha. So . . . as soon as I can get away from him. Can I . . . call you?"

"Yeah, yeah, sure."

"And I'm sorry about saying all that shit about loving you and all. I didn't mean to stress you out. You know, I'm just—"

"It's okay," Calhoun says. "Well, see you tomorrow."

"Yeah, uh . . . bye." Ziggy hangs up, moans, positive he's stressed Calhoun out. He opens his fist, and watches the Baggie unwind crookedly on his palm. It's intact, powder sparkling inside. It reminds him of . . . what? A smashed-down snow dome or whatever. Pretty. "Ziggy, you're such a fucking *loser,*" he whispers, glancing forlornly at a nearby trash can. If he tossed the Baggie in that direction, he could conceivably make a basket, but . . . Seconds later, he shoves the thing into his back pocket—"Shit"—then hits the sidewalk, thumb already out.

*C*alhoun stares into his desk's open drawer. At a glance, it's a mess—six, seven majestic if well-used syringes obscured by a flattened-out cloud bank of bloody cotton balls, blackened spoons, gummed-up cellophane squares . . . To Calhoun, it's a relatively organized kit.

Things don't have to be cordoned off in pockets, drawers, towns, neighborhoods, etc., to function. There's the possibility of genius in chaos, in having to fumble around, knowing whatever you need isn't all that well hidden a half-foot in any direction. But . . . Calhoun's accidentally caught sight of his arms, spotlit horrendously well by the desk lamp's wide spill. Jabbed to shit, they legitimize him in a way. Others reemerge from various parts of the world tanned and bubbling with tales one's heard millions of times. Someday he'll be able to roll up his sleeves and half-grin, Mona Lisa–like, while people wonder and worry a little in retrospect. These arms are *his*, like the moon is a handful of astronauts'. Subliminally numb all the time, streaked with collapsed, ashen veins, they've begun to repel needles' pricks, no matter how fine the implement. Locating a usable vein requires eight or nine pokes as of earlier today. He's even been forced into poking the backs of his hands, which are noticeably puffed up and blanched. Studying them, he feels a dull, far-off sadness, which, right on fucking cue, his dimming high turns into spaciness before he can drift into too much analysis. Through heroin, Calhoun has found the kind of questionable comfort and amorality he needs to survive, for a while anyway. But it's too typical and ironic, he thinks, that love—since *love* is just how the thing between heroin and him reads, based on his limited info—would finally enter what's left of his life all enmeshed with this . . . this . . . —he looks at the drawer's sort of volcanic contents, then at his unfocused, inflated hands struggling to stay aloft in the foreground—this . . .

Osamu had conked out a few minutes back. I was gazing on him with extremely mixed feelings. Luckily he reeked of sex, particularly his much-explored ass, the smeared crack of which seemed to radiate nose-tingling spiciness, like something I'd just slid bubbling from an oven. As I crouched by the teenager, sniffing that garbagey reek—and preparing to hustle him out my front door—I must say I felt a very strange, even indescribable poignance.

"Osamu," I said. The boy opened his eyes, scared at first, then apparently pleased to be sprawled where he was sprawled. Soon he was happily regrinding his by-that-point-understood ass into my still mildly overwhelmed face.

Fifteen minutes later we lay side by side, spoiled, tired, frazzled. "Osamu," I said again. The boy was doing some kind of dancery lying-down leg exercises.

We discussed what had happened and what was potentially forthcoming re: us. I could have been much more straightforward, okay, but Osamu seemed so, well, positive about us as a couple. More to the point, I couldn't risk alienating him, since his folks could've technically called the police. So I persuaded the boy to take a compromise. In short, I wouldn't just cancel my flight to L.A. there and then, as Osamu was urging; I would guarantee that, if worst came to worst, I'd be equally true to the "boy in the West" *and* my guest.

Relatively satisfied, Osamu took a long shower while I stuffed a suitcase.

Maybe I was imagining things, but when the boy left my bathroom, he seemed to be strutting his stuff, as they say. There was a curious tilt to the towel he'd fixed round his waist, and it rode his hips far too precariously. Still, this lurid display was so totally unlike the Osamu I knew that I had to observe him for several minutes before I was sure.

"You're a slut," I announced mock accusingly. He was back in the bathroom again, blow-drying his hair with the door wide open.

Osamu claimed he was a virgin.

I accused him of cockiness.

Osamu said he was just happy.

As a rule, teenaged skin lulls me, nicely offsetting my intellectual response with its peacefulness. Osamu's skin followed suit, coming to rest—hovering really—around his bright musculature, not to mention the loveliest skeleton in New York, with such innate modesty that I *had* to repossess it that instant.

I entered the bathroom, ripping away Osamu's towel. The boy turned, smiled, triumphant. He told me something on the order of, use me however you wish, in a

defiant tone that I assumed had popped out of some rock
song or movie, as it was both fraught and a little clichéd.

I commandeered the blow dryer, switched it off,
dragged the giggling teenager back to my bed, posed him,
and spread his asscheeks so wide the ass lost its division
entirely, becoming a perfect, grayish brown ball, albeit
with the most luxurious and harshest-smelling puncture
in the world.

Bzzz, goes Calhoun's doorbell. He's just done his
shot, and is amdist an impeccable nod, but, guessing
who's probably out there, he clutches the chair's arms,
and, sniffling, propels himself into his messy room. Momentum carries him to the little intercom unit, which,
luckily, he painted an eye-stabbing red in tribute to his
oft-seen blood. "Yeah?" he asks, out of breath, pushing
the TALK button. As he'd hoped, prayed even, it's Annie's
unmistakable twang at the other end. "Come on in," he
says, holding the DOOR button down for a fairly long time.
Then he weaves through the halls and byways of his loft
to the main entrance/exit. Hurling open the thick metal
door, he squints. Here Annie struts with her boyish attire
and that big, goofy grin wherein he used to want to bury
his cock. Not that it's not still a reasonably delectable
thought, just a spacier one. It's up to her now. If she
suggests sex, he'll try to fulfill his daydream, as impotent

as heroin has left him of late. "Hey," he says. They wander into Calhoun's spacious, disheveled room. Is Annie smiling at him really warmly? Seems so. She strolls around, eyeing his paltry if beloved collection of bad thrift-store paintings. She's just sold some heroin to Ziggy McCauley, she says. "Yeah, he called me." Calhoun takes his usual seat. Ziggy sure does adore you, she adds. Calhoun nods. "He's a good friend." Anyway, she says, reaching around in her pocket, here's your dope. Calhoun accepts the profferred Baggie, and pulls out six twenties. She stashes them, then, unexpectedly, stands about a foot from his chair, her weight shifting from Doc Marten to Doc Marten, sort of . . . leering at him, it appears. Here's where in the old days he'd have thought about making a delicate suggestion. "Uh," he says, and tries to leer back complexly. "So . . ." Calhoun can't find the words. Even so, he wouldn't know how to give them a requisite comical spin, he's so zoned. Fuck other people, he thinks, sulking. Bitch. He's close to tears, not that it shows. Bored is how Calhoun's unhappiness reads. Tick, tick, tick, tick . . . Well, you take care, she mumbles reluctantly it seems, and heads for the door. Calhoun wants to say, Stay, or something to that effect. Instead, his mouth just sort of falls open, hangs there, a reddish black, roughly triangular slot, at the far back of which are some inventive emotions that don't have a chance against the shit heroin throws over everything in the world except its own . . . whatever. Slam.

* * *

Robin scratched at his gag.

Ken switched off the camera. "Shit," he said. Filling an old hypodermic with clear liquid sedative crap he'd had sitting around in a bottle for years, he pushed a sparkly drop out the tip and jabbed the Metal kid's shoulder.

Slayer's tape was white noise, to Ken's mind anyway, but if the kid liked it . . .

Robin, scared, woozy, lost, immobile, period.

Back at the video camera, Ken slowly zoomed in on the kid's reeking butt.

Giant butt in the foreground. Unfocused, Britishy face in the distance. Great shot.

Robin saw what he could manage to see.

"My nephew's on his way over," Ken said, in case Robin could hear. "That's my hurry."

Then Ken butt-fucked the kid, who just lay there all tensed.

Luckily Robin's face seemed like he was mentally into it, thanks to the drugs, no doubt.

"You're weird," Ken said, imitating Ziggy's voice maybe.

Good old Slayer.

Good old drugs.

Robin, pinned on his back, legs folded up, fat man balanced about an inch overhead like a teetering boulder, really fucking, *hard*, sweat dripping down, plip, plip, plip, on the kid's perky face.

Then the doorbell cut faintly through Slayer's LP.

"Shit," Ken said, climbed off the kid.

Robin opened his eyes a slit, saw light.

Ken was dressing. "My nephew," he yelled over the onslaught.

Ziggy punches Ken's bell, but the one-story house might as well be a giant, eccentric amplifier. It's shivery from the force of some dumb Heavy Metal the guy or his guest has cranked up. So Ziggy reaches up, locates the key Ken hides under the petrified shit in his birdhouse. Yuck. Click, click, cre-ea-ea-ak. "Uncle Ken!" he yells, mouth cupped. The living room's usually neat to the point of psychosis. Today the rug's hilly and spattered with wide-open porn magazines, not to mention innumerable small-ish, twisted articles of clothing. Budweiser cans line both arms of the fake-tartan couch, or, rather, couch bed, since its usual seat cushion's an unmade queen bed. Weird. Nobody's in the john, kitchen. That's obvious from here. But the Sex Hole's door's closed, not sitting open an orangy slit, as per most visits. So Ziggy does like he does when Ken's doing whatever he, ha ha ha, *does* in the Hole, and turns off the stereo system, to let the guy know he's present. . . . *A cannibal's desire feeds the fire that burns in your*—Click. Ziggy loves how, like, even after it's off, loud

music, especially guitar, hangs around in the air tinkling
faintly for two, three seconds. "Cool." It reminds him of
. . . what? He scrunches his face up. "Hm." Just about the
time that . . . ear ghost or whatever is burning off, Ken,
who always makes Ziggy think of that actor Ned
Beatty—but fatter, for sure, and with a dated shag haircut—throws back the door of the Hole, slams it behind
him, and stumbles into the living room, dressed in black
jeans and a tight blue T-shirt with red, white, and black
polka dots, looking fifty pounds heavier than even last
visit if possible, not to mention unusually trashed, on the
surface at least. He drops on the couch bed. It squeaks
wildly under his weight, thin metal legs slamming the
floor. Several beer cans fall off, pummeling the rug. Clunk,
clunk, clunk . . . clunk. A little beer mixed with soggy
tobacco or pot oozes out of one can near Ken's bare, hairy
feet. He just sits there, hunched over, while air explodes
in-out his mouth, and beer spreads in an octopusish
pattern.

"Your shirt's backwards," Ziggy says, leaning back
on the TV, a little dazed by everything.

Ken just watches the beer move. "Yeah," he manages. "I threw this on. In case you changed your mind and
brought Calhoun."

Ziggy sets his jaw—pissed, jealous, *something*. "So
the Heavy Metal kid's in there?" He nods cursorily in the
general direction of the room where things happen, which
means he has to look past this huge, framed poster of
naked kids swimming around in a lake that some sup-

posedly famous dead German photographer traded with
Ken for some rare kiddie porn.

"So, how *is* Calhoun?" Ken asks, zoned.

"He's *fine*," Ziggy says. "Well, he's kind of heavy
into heroin now, so that's, uh . . . a big worry, but . . ."
Ken nods vaguely off in the distance. "Anyway, you don't
care, fuck it." Ziggy kicks at the rug.

"Have you slept with him yet?" Ken mumbles.

"No!" Ziggy yells, a little too insistently maybe.
"That's not . . . I mean I wouldn't mind, but he's really,
really straight, so . . . and it doesn't *matter!*"

Ken's still studying the beer, his fat—to put it simplistically—face unfocused into a low-grade stare. "We
have to deal with some details," he says. "I'm making a
porno. Right now." He nods at the Sex Hole.

"Figured." Ziggy looks at the Hole too, meaning a
closed door.

"So, I'm in a strange place."

Ziggy squints at the door's folksy, hand-lettered
sign, *Gone Fishin'*, ha ha ha. Ken's news is too loaded to
process. Anyway, Ziggy's mostly curious about the Metal
kid, who he is, how he looks, what his take is on being in
porn, not to mention the Hole itself, which Ziggy hasn't
seen firsthand for . . . God, it's been *years*. "Can the kid
. . . talk?" Ziggy asks.

"Talk?" Ken sits forward, making his face slop
around on his skull a bit. Yuck. "Well, he's gagged. But,
yeah, a little. Why?"

Ziggy's eyes unfocus slightly. "Would it freak me
out to see him?"

"I don't know," says Ken's voice.

"Is the Sex Hole locked up?" Ziggy shoves a fingertip between his teeth and starts gnawing the crescent of skin that frames its very bitten-down nail.

"No, but—"

Ziggy nods furiously, already up on his feet, halfway across the room. He twists the doorknob, throws the Hole wide open, squints. So . . . It's still a barely furnished little movie set. Same double bed on a platform, cheap covers, end table, lamp, very motellike in theory, except now, unlike in Ziggy's day, there's a videocam on a tripod midroom, as opposed to a super 8 camera, and the ceiling, once plunked with a single spotlight, is an upside-down trainyard of track lights, all their bulbs aimed at the bed, where a short, skinny, bleached-out, nude kid's lying flat on his back—microscopic genitalia, eyes shut, mouth hanging open, legs together, arms clamped to his sides militarily. His chest is so sunken he looks like a human canoe. Also, he's more, well, skinhead than Heavy Metal until, that is, Ziggy realizes the gag in his mouth is a twist of long, blond—if obviously dyed—human hair. *"All right, Uncle Ken,"* Ziggy whispers, half impressed, half sort of horrified. He's standing there, hands bunched in pockets, looking around, when the kid's eyelids part about a quarter inch, blink several times, fixing on . . . Ziggy?

"Shit. Uh, hi," Ziggy says. "I'm the nephew of, uh, Ken. But I'm neutral. I'm not into this stuff in the same way he is. I . . . come in peace, ha ha ha."

The kid seems amazingly gone. Like if his brain had

been slipped out the back so his eyeballs had nothing worthwhile to report.

"You're tired. That's cool. I dig." Ziggy takes a couple of steps toward the kid, hands out to show he's not holding a weapon. "It's intense to see you. People are so weird. Especially Uncle Ken, as you know." He smirks tentatively.

The kid doesn't respond.

Ziggy reburies his hands in his jeans pockets, toes the wooden floor, careful to avoid a minigalaxy of . . . it looks like sperm driplets. "This is totally insensitive of me, isn't it? I'm really bad about knowing when to censor myself. Everyone says so. Sorry." He glances up from his shoe.

Staring, gagged, unreadable kid.

"Actually," Ziggy continues. "The reason I'm here is to see if I can handle your predicament first of all, which I guess I can, and then to ask you some questions. Because I publish this magazine about, like, sexual abuse, and an interview with you would be an amazing coup." Ziggy cringes, knowing how flip that sounds.

The kid's just sort of looking at Ziggy, eyes full of . . . who-knows-what, skin so consistently sweaty he seems cast in resin. But sexy. Ziggy's cock's gotten hard just from studying the situation. Shit. He fiddles with it worriedly, trying to figure out whose side he's on at the moment. Probably the kid's, but . . . Now something among his thoughts gels, though it's more like he's realizing he's realizing something than . . . whatever . . . a revelation.

"Just a second, okay? Sorry." He smiles at the kid, whirls around, runs to the door, and sticks his head into the living room. "Uncle Ken!" he yells.

Ken looks up from . . . the rug? Maybe he's still obsessing about the spilled Budweiser. "Yeah, what?" he asks softly. "Trouble?"

Ziggy shakes his head. "Can you come in here? I want to interview you and the kid at the same time. For *I Apologize*. Isn't that a brilliant idea?"

Ken's already in the process of standing. "Okay," he says between gasps and grunts. "If it's . . . no, wait." He tips back on the couch bed, making its springs creak hysterically. "You print that it's fiction." He points at Ziggy. "That you made it up." The finger wiggles. "That it's your fucked-up fantasy."

"Sure, sure, sure, sure." Ziggy's dancing around on his toes.

"It *is* an amusing idea." Ken grunts. He struggles back up to his feet, a labored process that Ziggy's gotten used to, but it always seems like there should be opera playing while it happens or something.

"Come *on*," Ziggy squeals. "Bring some paper and pens. This is going to be *so cool*." He spins around, lurches back into the Hole; straight at the kid, putting on the brakes just in time. "This is okay with you, right?" Ziggy asks Robin, easing down on the bed's edge.

The kid just looks at or through Ziggy with this seeming horror that one almost never gets to see, except in documentaries.

In the background a door clicks shut. Ken takes a breath that could easily be Hurricane Whoever edited down to a sound bite and lumbers to where Ziggy's sitting. In his hands are paper, pen. "I can . . ." Ken leans over the kid, who just stares back, irises colorless as magnets. ". . . inject him with speed," Ken continues. "If you're serious about the interview. That'll reenergize him. Because he's Mr. Sedatives at the moment."

"Sure, great!" Ziggy's tapping his foot. "But it won't, like, hurt him any more than he's already hurt, will it? Please say no, ha ha ha."

Ken shakes his head, which makes his face wave around on his well-hidden skull again. *Yuck*. He's traded the paper and pen for a syringe, and is already pushing a drop of translucent liquid out the tip. "There's a remote possibility," he says, sticking the needle into one of the kid's scrawny biceps, "that it'll denumb him a little." The hypodermic fills up with blood, then that's pushed out. "But supposedly . . . *there*"—and he withdraws the needle—"parts of the brain blow a fuse in these situations. And it doesn't completely repair until . . . six, eight months of therapy later, if then." Ken lays the empty works down on the night table prop. "But *you* tell *me*, Ziggy." He grins. "*You're* the *expert*."

Is it Ziggy's imagination or has the Metal kid's face grown both friendlier and less cute postneedle? It's like the difference between how forgettable that young actor, Corey What's-it, looked sitting in court on the news yesterday, as opposed to how faraway and ideal he used to seem in his films like *The Lost Boys*. Anyway . . . "Uh, so is it okay to do this weird interview thing?" Ziggy looks warily at the kid.

Robin makes a sound that maybe could've been a yes.

"Scary," Ziggy mumbles to himself, and gives Ken a long, meaningful look that says, Untie the gag, yeah?

"Meet Robin," announces Ken. He takes some rumbly breaths, and starts undoing the gag. "Thirteen years old. Favorite band, Slayer." He's toying with a knot. ". . . and . . . that's . . . all . . . I . . ." The gag loosens, flops down on the pillow, sliding bit by bit over the mattress's brim in a long, unbroken line, as if it's slithering off to locate a new victim. But as soon as this "snake" hits the floor, it immediately spreads out into a shabby mat.

"Fuck *you*," Robin says, glaring at both of them. His voice is all phlegmy, but under that crass decoration is the flat, high-pitched voice that makes parents all over the world so irritable supposedly. His shaved head lifts up, trembling, but his body stays limp, like it's just his foundation.

Ken's rejoined Ziggy now.

Robin gulps down air, his glistening, greenish white skin rising, falling around a treacherous-looking if sort of delicate skeleton.

Ziggy shields his lips. "So, Uncle Ken," he whispers, and gets a snootful of his own breath, which has gone really sour. "Are you finished with the filming?"

"Let's ask him," Ken whispers back. "Robin! Anything left to figure out about you?"

Robin looks at Ken blankly, as far as Ziggy can tell,

but there are probably codes galore passing between them. "I . . . don't know, man," he says.

"Might as well go ahead, Ziggy." Ken grabs the writing implements off the bedside table and hands them to his nephew. "Because I'm tired, Robin's *definitely* tired."

"Right." Ziggy braces a page in one hand, clicks and lowers the pen. Even slight pressure buckles the sheet. So Ken slogs out to the living room, slogs back, and hands him a coffee table book on the Impressionists to use as support. All of this takes about a minute and a half, during which Ziggy looks at everything except the kid, meaning the camera, walls, chair . . . "Okay," he continues. "I might not actually print this part. It's mostly to get us, like, going." He starts doodling a spiral. "Uh, Robin, when you came to my uncle's last night, what did you think was going to happen?"

The kid's eyes—which, to this point, have resembled small, unfocused geodes—sharpen, filling with . . . intelligence? Weird. They're actually a nice dark brown color, even with all the chemicals probably blowing their wiring or whatever. "He . . .," the kid says. Robin peers at Ken. ". . . was gonna pay me for sex."

"Okay." Ziggy's writing away. "Got . . . it . . . And, uh, when did you realize that something was . . . weird?"

Robin's eyes go all starey, bypassing Ken, but when Ziggy turns to see what's in the way, there's just the more boring part of the room, and . . . oh, right, a framed movie poster for *Home Alone*, featuring a screaming child actor whom Robin remotely resembles. Hm. "He got me stoned," Robin says in the background. There's something very odd about the poster. "And I thought, What if he gives me AIDS?" Maybe it's just the fake fear on the young actor's face and how offensive that is at the moment or something. "And then . . ." Robin swallows noisily. ". . . you started saying how . . ." Ziggy forces his eyes back to the Metal kid's face, which is staring at Ken now. *That's* terror, Ziggy thinks, studying the contorted expression. ". . . how you were in love with me." Down on his chest, Robin's hands knot together and . . . vibrate?

"You mean, how you were gorgeous." Ken's just plopped down on a folding chair over by the camera.

Robin winces.

"That wasn't *love.*" Ken chokes out a sluggish rivulet of breath. "Jesus . . . you're . . . so . . . ." He wags his head. Slop, slop.

"But Uncle Ken," Ziggy says. "You *do* get all passionate about boys, so Robin could've easily thought you were hot for him. He didn't *know.*"

"I *was* hot. I *am.*" Ken breathes out again, but his body's so fucked up it could be a laugh or a cough. "But, come on, love? That's too liberal." He leans forward, grabs the chest part of his T-shirt, gasps. "You pick a kid out of the zillions of them . . ." Gas-as-as-asp. ". . . you risk prison to fuck him . . ." A couple more gasps. ". . . that's *like* love, *okay.* But Robin means *love.* Boyfriends, life companions, *that* nonsense." And Ken leans back, folds his hands in his lap, breathing as normally as he ever does.

"No, no," Robin says, voice sort of husky and

thinned to a wisp at the same time. His hands hammer down on his chest. "I mean . . ." His face sort of lengthens and freezes there, quivering in places, no longer even remotely good looking, as far as Ziggy can tell. ". . . I mean you were . . . *in love.*" He swings the hammer up to his lips. They're wiggling frantically. He's having a hard time not screaming or something.

Ken exhales paranormally and doesn't say anything.

Ziggy flips over the page. "Which is it more like, Uncle Ken, love or hate?"

"Neither," the man barks. "This kid's just got a *prehistoric* take on the world thanks to the *stupid* lyrics of that *band* he's so into. It's like . . . Ziggy, *you* know what this is like."

"Wait, ha ha ha," Ziggy says, scribbling that down. "Uh, maybe. Listen, do you remember Roger, Brice's ex-boyfriend? Well, he's definitely like you are with kids, but about young guys' asses. It's so *weird*, Uncle Ken." He stops writing for a moment. "Roger's flying out here from New York tomorrow, and he's going to move me back East with him."

"No shit," Ken says.

In the near distance, Robin's still freaking out in a taut, quiet way that's subtle but hard to ignore.

"It's true!" Ziggy grins. But then he glances at miserable Robin and warms, discolors, etc., in embarrassment. "So anyway." He repositions his pen. "Uh . . . what kind of sex did you have with Robin?"

"Good question." Ken's eyes jitter around like his thoughts are rewinding.

Ziggy waits, flexing his cramped right hand, but Ken's eyes just keep jittering. "Well, uh . . . I'm gonna need some more paper, if you have some. I mean, if you're having trouble remembering." Still jittering, period. "So, Uncle Ken, uh . . . it looks like you've changed your technique since the, ha ha ha, old days."

At that Ken awakes, stands, stumbles into the living room. Sound of drawers opening, closing. A few seconds later he's back with a fresh piece of paper for Ziggy. "I've refined some," he says, handing it over. "If you watch the movie of you, then the video of Robin, you can tell."

"Maybe later." Ziggy checks up on Robin, who's partway back into his fogged-out, original, sexier state. "Uncle Ken, let me ask Robin stuff now, because he's fading again or whatever."

Ken sits down on the chair again, crack, squeak, and squints at the kid.

"Robin?" Ziggy asks loudly. "Uh, what were you thinking about during the sex part? I mean, *at the time.*"

The kid, whose sweaty face has started to look, well, deformed, raises his eyelids a fraction, the right one especially. A teensy flickerette of energy appears deep inside it. "Shomeshing," he mumbles.

"*Fuck,* Uncle Ken," Ziggy croaks. "Robin's not going to O.D., is he?" He holds the art book in front of his face just in case.

"It's nothing," says Ken.

Ziggy peeks over the edge of the book. Robin's seemingly okayish still. "So was it . . ."—Ziggy lowers the book, paper, pen, and starts doodling in a frenzy—". . . just horrifying? Like you'd expect something like that would have been? Uh, *Robin?*" Ziggy wants to look up, but . . . he can't.

After what feels like three or four minutes, the kid's voice says, "I . . . don't know."

"Did hearing Slayer's music help?" Doodle, doodle.

Ziggy carefully raises his eyes, and, weird, the old Robin's back again, or at least the "old Robin" Ziggy's gotten to know, meaning his face is very, very mellow but not, like, a corpse's.

"I *did* hear it." Robin looks over at Ziggy, uh . . . hopefully? Weird.

"Did it sound as high quality as you thought?"

"Yeah." Robin nods. His face has begun to sort of glimmer again. It's actually surprisingly cute, in an obvious, TV star's way. "Tom . . . Araya's lyrics are so . . . true."

"Wait," Ziggy blurts, floored. "Are you . . . *are you* saying that Slayer made it easier to endure the, uh, rape and all that? I mean, knowing how good Slayer is?"

Robin's head shakes, not in any particular direction. Probably a nod. Whuff, whuff, whuff, goes the pillow.

"This is amazing." Ziggy writes furiously. His script has decayed to the unreadable stage. "So you decided that Slayer's music's good enough that being raped isn't, like, uh . . . important?"

"That's . . . yeah," Robin says, and his eyes sort of jab out.

"It's so *bizarre*, Uncle Ken." Ziggy glances back at the man, who's just sitting there, bulbous arms X-ing his belly. "You don't think so?"

Ken shakes his head sort of vaguely, then stops, reaches up, gives a scratch to that spooky shag haircut, like he's reconsidering the question.

"Actually, *that's* amazing *too*. I mean that you're not sure. Wow." Ziggy scribbles a note to himself. But when he turns around, checks up on Robin again, something's new. The kid's brown eyes are crossed, as if he's trying to look into the pores on his nose. And he's swallowing so often his neck's a tornado. "Uh, Robin?"

"Maybe he *is* sick." Ken stands laboriously and heads for the bed. "Finish up."

"Okay." Ziggy doodles. "*I* don't know. Shit, Uncle Ken." He peers around the room, desperate for inspiration. The *Home Alone* poster's already conveyed everything it could convey. "Well, then, Robin, uh . . ." He looks at the kid, who's turned a strange color . . . yellowy blue? "Does it matter to you that, uh, Uncle Ken thinks you're, uh, really beautiful?"

"No . . ." Robin's voice is a squawk. "I know . . . I'm . . ." The Metal kid's eyes have gotten so . . . well, frightened doesn't quite cover it, that Ziggy clutches his throat to keep from crying or yelling, he can't tell.

Ken takes about seven steps backwards, which shoots a wave of B.O. through the room. Ugh.

Robin tries to roll onto his side several times, can't, whips his head to the right, making his neck twist into this huge, crude rope, and vomits a lumpy mush across the pillow, then just lies there, burnt, gasping.

The room starts to smell of . . . stomach acid?

"You've got to go," Ken says, pinching his nose shut. "I have to decide what to do."

"I dig." Ziggy fans the air. "But you have to let me ask what you're thinking." He points at what's left of Robin. "I mean, 'cos he's, like, gross now, so . . ." Ziggy has to let his fanning/writing arm fall to his side, it's so used up and achy.

"I'm letting him register," Ken says. "If that makes any sense."

Ziggy copies that down. "Maybe. Like when you love someone, you don't mind the gross parts. They're just . . . part of the bargain." Ziggy scratches his filthy hair. "That's what my school therapist says."

"Close." Ken's huge face twists in two or three directions at once if that's possible. "Phew!" He staggers out of the Hole.

"Except," Ziggy shouts after him, fanning again. "Well, you raped and whatever someone who maybe didn't deserve it!" Ziggy bunches his lips, still scratching, weighing positives and negatives. "And is that . . . cool?"

"There are a lot of human beings," Ken bellows from the living room.

"Yeah, so?" Ziggy eyes Robin, who's either asleep now or praying, then eyes Ken, or, more specifically, a shadow. That shadow and Robin are like . . . polar opposites? Note. "What does *that* have to do with anything?"

"Selectivity," yells Ken's voice. "Choose a couple of friends . . . Everyone else is just there." It sounds like he's straightening up. "Not your or my problem . . . So if Robin's been fucked psychologically . . . *I* won't know. That's a theory . . . But I had a great time. I did. And . . . Robin's not quite . . . intelligent enough to . . . be of interest to anyone other than . . . sex maniacs like myself . . . Because unless you're fixated on druggies . . . he's not worth the hassle."

Ziggy knows he should've written that down, but he's brain dead. "Can I borrow the Slayer tape?" he manages to yell. "Do you think he'd mind?" He nods at Robin, who's probably still too nauseous to care what's going on. "I want to transcribe the lyrics. Hey, Uncle Ken! You never know, they might add . . . color?"

"Sure, whatever." Ken slams a door somewhere.

Ziggy folds the several-page interview, slipping it into his blue jeans' back pocket. He heads out to the living room, which seems to have this weird, homey quality he never noticed before. The bed being there helps, obviously. So he pauses for a few seconds, yawning. Tick, tick . . . He pops Ken's cassette deck, removes the Slayer tape, jamming same into his jacket's stuffed pocket, clack, clack, and glances back at the open Sex Hole. The vomity odor is filtering out.

"Bye, Uncle Ken," he shouts, already through the front door. "Talk to you tomorrow! This was . . . interesting!"

From deep inside the house there's a muffled flush.

*R*obin could . . . focus . . . his eyes . . . but . . .

When the fat man reentered the Sex Hole to clean up their mess, he realized the extent and practically crushed his nose shut.

"You didn't," Ken said.

Around Robin's bare hips, thighs, the very first fringe of a creeping brown stain.

"Take a shower," the fat man yelled. He grabbed the kid's wrist, yanked. Robin stumbled out of bed, fell to his knees, took a few screechy breaths. "Apologies," Ken added.

"I'm . . . okay," Robin said.

Then Ken ripped up the soggy bedding and bunched it. He unlatched a window, heaved-ho, and in-haled some cold night. In his peripheral vision, the kid crawled away.

Shower noise, whish, like an auditory eraser, whish, removed a little bit of the experience, whish, for the kid anyhow.

Robin lay crookedly under the hot, itchy jets. "My . . . hair," he said, gripping the rim of the bathtub. He missed its gentle weight on his shoulders. "Fuck." After a second he picked up the soap.

Ken mopped for a half hour, whistling.

The air in the Sex Hole got better and better and better.

The kid limped to Ken's living room, nude, drippy, located clothes, dressed himself.

"I've made your check out to Barry," the fat man said, watching the kid hide his body. "He'll cash it."

"Can I . . .?" asked Robin. He stood there, fists clenched. ". . . crash here? Just till tomorrow?" He made his eyes look distraught, if they had any powers left in them, that is.

The fat man nodded, then yawned at great length.

" 'Cos I'm too tired to—"

"All right." The kid's beauty had sort of returned with his clothes, though it definitely seemed weaker. "But I can't guarantee I won't . . ."

Robin nodded frantically. That's when he missed his long hair most of all for some reason.

"Do a striptease," Ken said. "Reinvent yourself."

"What?" asked the kid.

The fat man drew in the air with a finger, some kind of violent squiggle, maybe clothes flying around. "Then we'll crash."

Robin whipped off his T-shirt, stood there, panting, already exhausted.

"Slo-o-o-o-wer," Ken said.

The kid slowed.

*P*unching the doorbell three times, Ziggy peeps through the little square grate to the left of the buttons, where Calhoun's soothing voice will waft out, if he's around or awake. There's a spiderweb in there.

"Uh . . . hello?"

"It's me," Ziggy says, almost kissing the apparatus. "You up?"

"Sort of, yeah." The web's fluttering gently. "I'll let you in."

The metal gate vibrates, whirrs, and Ziggy shoves his way through. Halfway down the former toy factory's dark central hall, he sees a slanted light, triangle shaped, with a dim, black, elongated blob wavering in the middle like a ghostly chocolate center or an X ray. That must be Calhoun's shadow. Seconds later, yeah, his best friend's mussed-up blond hair and sort of Quakerish features jut out a doorway.

"Hey," Calhoun says, blinks.

"I know you hate to hear this," Ziggy says, rushing up to him. "But, God, I'm so glad to see you. You don't *know.*"

Calhoun makes one of his fake perturbed faces, so instead of hugging him, which is Ziggy's first thought, they scoot into the loft. Even Calhoun's walk—tense, shuffling, back stiff, arms pumping rigidly at his sides—make Ziggy grin really happily. When Calhoun turns, seems to notice, Ziggy bites away signs of his pleasure, but not in time, it appears.

"What?" Calhoun half-grins. He eases down in his desk chair.

Ziggy sprawls on the bed. "Nothing. Just the usual glad-to-be-with-you stuff."

Calhoun nods nervously.

"When *do* you sleep?" Ziggy asks, sitting up.

"Shortly." Calhoun's pupils are so tiny from the heroin they're like microdots of the *Encyclopaedia Britannica* or whatever.

"Well, you won't believe what just happened." Ziggy grabs his knees, shaking them around. "I was at my psycho uncle's. You know, the one who made that video I lent you? And he had this kid there—I forget his name—uh . . . doing a video, and I interviewed him—well, him *and* Uncle Ken, but my uncle wasn't as interesting since I already know *him*. And I'm gonna print it in *I Apologize*. 'Cos it was amazing! I think I'm gonna do a bunch of interviews. Maybe I'll do one with you."

Calhoun's listening, mouth crumpled, visage otherwise blank if enlivened by occasional blinks and sniffles.

"Would that be okay?"

Calhoun scratches his nose. "Yeah, I guess. But what do I have to do with it?"

"Well," Ziggy says, sort of surgically removing wordage from his brain. "Because . . . you're the antidote to all that. When I'm with you, it's weird how okay all the horrible parts seem. Like it's all just some interesting stuff I can tell you about. Really. The only times I feel good are when I'm working on *I Apologize* or when I'm with you." He smiles beatifically.

"Ziggy, Jesus," Calhoun mutters, and saws the back of one hand across his nose. "I like seeing you too. You're my best friend, but . . ." He gives his lap an agonized look. ". . . and I don't mean to offend. Still, why do you always want to talk about our friendship? Why can't it just happen? I mean, I know how you feel. Trust me."

Horrified, Ziggy laughs, but it's an ugly honk thing. "Yeah, yeah, yeah. I'm too verbal, I know. The school therapist says I'm, uh . . . I'm afraid if I don't tell you I like you all the time—oh, 'cos I told her how important our friendship is now—that you'll have a reason to reject me. But she says it works the opposite way, and, uh, that I'm really just trying to make it impossible for you to say how you feel about me, 'cos I'm afraid what you'll say is I don't really matter to you. But I told her, 'No, our friendship's really mutual back and forth.' " He looks up hopefully. "That's what's so brilliant about it, that we're so bonded."

"Yeah," says Calhoun. His eyes seem like they're aimed through Ziggy's chest at some infinite point. "I don't know . . . I guess I don't want to be that close to people."

Ziggy nods, but it feels really stiff. "Don't you

think maybe you *do* like how close we are now, you just can't think about it too much, like you said?"

"I don't know." Calhoun's still staring way out . . . wherever. "I hate talking about this."

"Yeah, sorry." Terror, albeit mild, has weighed down Ziggy's head until he's watching Calhoun through the smoke of his unfocused eyebrows. "I understand. Uh . . ." He clears his throat. ". . . but I guess I sort of have to decide you do love me a lot, and you can't tell me so, 'cos . . . it'd be hard to go on if I didn't believe that. I know it sounds weird."

Calhoun nods, tips a cigarette out of the pack on his desktop, and uses his lighter on it. "Okay," he says through a smoke gust. The cigarette hand hits the arm of his desk chair and pats nervously a few times. He's forced a degree of warmth into his eyes from somewhere. They meet Ziggy's, and pass along something very close to reassurance.

"You mean so much to me, Calhoun," Ziggy whispers. But he has to glance away at a bad thrift-store painting of Venice to actually pronounce that. "You really do. But now I'll shut up. And, uh . . . we can talk about something else."

"You mean a lot to me too." Calhoun manages a . . . smirk? "But, you know, *shut up.*" His voice squeaks on the *up*.

"Right," Ziggy says, smashing his lips together.

Calhoun's smirk devolves into a grimace. He looks down, probably at the chunk of text glistening on the

screen of his laptop computer. Or he might be studying
the spare, nasty snowfall of bloodstained, crushed cotton
balls all around it. Or maybe it's the combination. Anyway, his face has this softness and poignance that starts
the idiotic emotion bomb ticking in Ziggy's chest, albeit a
tick so subtle that they could easily part before it goes off
or whatever.

"Guess what else?"

Calhoun enlarges his eyes, but they're still aimed
somewhere on the desk.

"I fucked this girl Nicole . . . I forget her last name.
Lampley or something? Do you remember her from
school?

"Yup. Nice-looking girl."

"Totally!"

"Congratulations."

"Yeah, she's cool. We'll, uh, *see what happens now*,
ha ha ha." Ziggy slugs the bed happily. Again.

Calhoun nods. "So, I should do my next hit and
crash," he says. He takes a drag on his cigarette.

"Right." Ziggy leaps to his feet, making both knee
joints crackle explosively. He jams his hands into his
pockets. "Uh, sorry."

"Oh, I got you a present." Calhoun reaches into his
shirt pocket and slides out a cassette without taking his
eyes off the desk. He holds it out. "I stole it from work."
He smiles dimly.

Ziggy glances at the tape, then snatches it like it's
worth multimultimulti-zillion dollars. "Wow! *Thanks,*

Calhoun." It's this new collection of Hüsker Dü rarities and outtakes. "I've been dying to hear this."

"So . . ." Calhoun rips his eyes away from the desk, meeting Ziggy's. Anytime their eyes lock, even accidentally, Ziggy's warmed and, well, honored, but this time his best friend's expression seems so, uh . . . disturbed by what has to be, *has* to be an emotion or serious thought about him that he feels kind of trapped, though he knows he could move around technically. ". . . See ya."

"Yeah," Ziggy says. "Uh . . . sleep well." He takes three stumbly steps backwards. "B-bye."

Sprawled on his back, Calhoun turns on the TV and watches a rerun of *Sanford and Son*. It keeps his eyes moving if not too much else. But it can't prevent them from veering down to those discolored arms. They crisscross his stomach, bulging out below the wrists like clowns' "hands," one plunked with an ashy cigarette. He needs to shove in a needle ere long. Yeah, where? He squints, raises his head, which feels . . . ticklish. No, nauseating. *Shit*. He has to give up this idiocy soon, horrified as he is of the rocky unhappiness he tells himself *was* his preheroin life. Still . . . the perfect drug hasn't successfully distanced, attenuated, and framed everything, provided the world with a laugh track, then let Calhoun zone on his bed, observing its inhabitants' antics. But it's not like his life has been downgraded either. Things aren't less

valuable exactly. It's more like addiction's funereal pace
has mediated or . . . quelled certain threatening aspects.
Where it used to be sleep's gentle weight on the eyelids
would sort of erase Calhoun's misery for eight to ten hours
at a time, nowadays dreams just compete awkwardly with
his high, in which the world doesn't have to go away to
improve. When heroin's out of his system, if ever, his
life'll be . . . what? He can't remember too well. Well, he'll
write again for one thing, and be a savvier friend, especially to Ziggy, whose irritating devotion, even when Calhoun's an asshole and virtual zombie, socially at least,
seems so uncalled for, inexplicable, and impossible to re-
ward at the moment, that he has to immediately deep-six
his eyes into the rerun—specifically Redd Foxx's character faking his eight billionth stroke or whatever—to keep
a nagging teardrop inside. He'd let it loose if he knew
where it came from. Not that there aren't numerous, really great reasons to cry. Just not now. At some future
point, he'll sort out this Ziggy, etc., shit and . . . whatever.
Calhoun sniffles. Make a note, he thinks.

*T*he Metal kid eased out from under a sleeping fat
arm. It dropped a half-foot but didn't wake what's-his-
name up.

Hands extended and trembling, way out in front of
him, a bald-headed kid negotiated the gray, jam-packed
house, roughly aimed at a tall, dim rectangle of kitchen.

"Ouch . . . fuck." Coffee table leg.

Deep, deep, deep, deep inside the fridge, behind beers, Coke, etc., Robin touched a plastic bag that didn't seem to belong there.

The kid held it up under the moonlit north window. "Oh, *yeah.*" Hypodermic, spoon, packet of . . . heroin or speed probably.

Robin's pixieish face in a flattering light.

A very tiny percolating soundtrack as the drug cooked.

The kid studied the veins in his arms. "Shit, shit, shit . . ." Then he noticed one in his left biceps as bluish and wide as a felt-tip pen mark.

Bodies, weird.

Needle's prick, blood seeping into the brown stuff, the mixture sluicing back into his system.

Then the kid laid down Ken's hypodermic and sta-a-a-ared at the great black outdoors.

"Whoa." The world started weaving around like . . . like . . .

Robin tripped fifteen times on his way to the bedroom, which barely existed to his hazed-out eyes.

Eyes shut, stumbling, the kid prayed to Tom Araya to help him . . . well, walk for one thing.

Robin, down on his knees, head thrown back, neck stretched as tight as a pup tent, emitted a noise like his throat had been cut.

But . . . he . . . made . . . it . . . to . . . to . . . the . . . the . . . the . . . bed.

"Man?" he said weakly. His hand spasmed once, twice.

Ken raised his head, eyes out of focus.

Moonlit kid's Britishy face with a . . . religious expression.

Tick, tick, tick . . .

Around the kid's body, a world almost totally erased. "Beautiful," Ken whispered.

Whoosh. The fat man's head flattened his pillow.

Robin: An almost inaudible death rattle.

Ken: "Snore."

"*T*hanks for the ride, ma'am," Ziggy says. Slam. He trots up his driveway. Dawn's more amazing than usual, maybe because Ziggy's such a psychological disaster. The sky changes color and cloud configuration so rapidly he starts to feel dizzy, so when the door jiggles open, he runs inside, even though he's already way breathless from lack of REM sleep before he picks up his pace. He immediately checks Brice's whereabouts. Gone, it would seem, since everywhere's vacant. Cool. Yeah, a note underneath an apple perched on the dining-room table reads, *Ziggy, Back Sunday night at the latest. Dad.* Scary handwriting, words twisted and bunched into scrawny haystacks. I should print this, like, what do they call it . . . facsimile, yeah . . . in *I Apologize*. Remember. Then Ziggy staggers to the phone machine, poking the button marked MESSAGES. "Three," the machine says robotically. Whirr, beep. "It's Ken, Ziggy. Ask your friend Calhoun to call me. Tell him I know a really great heroin dealer. Thanks." Beep. "Ziggy, it's Annie. Great deal on somethin' new. Call if you want it." Beep. "Hello, Ziggy? It's Nicole. I just wanted to say it was nice last night. Let's do it again. Call me." Beep, beep, beep. Ziggy grins immensely for a second, then pushes ERASE. He wanders, daydreamy, arms swinging around, into his wrecked room. "Shit." Luckily, exhaustion has softened its blow. He steps through the trash heaps, and topples back first onto his bed. Squeak, squeak. It's practically 7:00 A.M. The world's too dimmed, etc., by sleepiness to fully appreciate. So, rather than shortchange his thoughts about anything in particular, Ziggy sits up, undresses, sets what's-his-name's Slayer tape down on his cassette deck, then lowers the dust-caked venetian blinds over his bedroom's one window. He unseals Calhoun's gift, fits that tape into his deck, pushes PLAY, and flops down again. Ph-e-e-ew . . . *If I listened to the things that you said, everything would fall apart* . . . Exactly. "Calhoun, don't die," he whispers, picturing that pale, stoned-out face. *I won't. Get some sleep, Ziggy.* "Okay, pal." Ziggy yawns. "What a mess," he slurs, glancing around his destroyed room. 7:08 A.M. "Roger'll . . . think . . ." He yawns. "I'm . . ."

I dozed through most of the flight, waking up at a poke from the man in the window seat. He needed to pee.

Then I sleepily watched the last forty minutes or so—sans headphones—of *Leap of Faith*, starring Steve Martin as an evangelist/healer unsurprisingly bent on relieving midwesterners of their immediate cash. Fortunately for me, in one of the smaller roles there was a doe-eyed, big-eared, bee-sting-lipped, longish-haired teen actor who spent most of his on-screen time hobbling on crutches. In fact, there were so many shots of his laboring ass in close-up that I began to suspect the director's intentions.

Ahem. What *is* the source of my interest in asses? (This gets better. Wait.) So frequently lust wrests the power away from my intellect, and, ruminate as I might, I'm reduced to devising paeans, period, as though this worshipful predilection were common, which I presume it is not. I would hazard a guess that this little fixation involves an avoidance of more resolute body parts, namely the face and genitalia, both of which, while fascinating, present too much personality, thereby reinforcing my failure to penetrate the givens of people I crave. For, of the body's main features, an ass is the most vague in meaning and structurally flexible. What *is* an ass if not the world's best designed, most inviting blank space, on the one hand, and, on the other, a grungy peephole into humans' ordinariness, to put it mildly?

L.A. was entirely smogged over that morning, so I was denied the adrenaline rush of floating onto its endless and bleached teenaged-boy-peppered grid. I deplaned, crossed the airport, caught the car rental agency's minibus. Avis. After a torpid half hour of waiting in line, and superficially friendly blah-blah with an I.Q.-less employee, I shot away cramped in a red Honda Civic. An hour later, it and I whirred into the scrubby, arid San Gabriel Valley, whose flat neighborhoods were inexpensive enough for my brainless, job-flitting, assholish ex-boyfriend.

I'd visited Ziggy perhaps a half-dozen times over the last several years, always on weekends when Brice was off fucking—I should say fucking over—some boyfriend. A brief, pothole-dotted driveway led to a standard garage, shut, yellow paint flaking unchecked off the door. I parked there, lugging my suitcase toward the nondescript, fifties-style tract house. One huge tree of an indeterminate type cloaked maybe half of the building, casting an immense, rough parabola of shade, especially slanted and dark at this early hour. I was grateful for it, since a slight trembling had begun to interfere with my movements, and worrying how Ziggy might misinterpret this nervousness left a discernible sparkle of sweat on my forehead.

"*F*uck, *hold on*," Ziggy yells over the doorbell's mind-boggling clangs. He plods down the hall, quasi-dressed in a Hüsker Dü T-shirt, period, one hand stretching its hem down, down, down over his flip-floppy genitals. Half to three-quarters asleep, he yanks open the front door. With his free hand, he shields his hazed eyes against the blindingly lighted outdoors.

"Hello, angel," says Roger's voice. First the guy's just some wavering shade sort of doused in fluorescence, but, as Ziggy's pupils do their mysterious adjustments, his visitor crisps into focus.

"Uh . . . yeah. Hi." It's weird, Ziggy thinks. Maybe his dad's gotten older and heavier over the weeks, make that months, since they last hung around, but the "Roger" he's been imagining to jerk off and the Roger he has to accept as, like, fact, as of now, could be . . . son and father?

"So it begins," Roger half-says, half- . . . moans? His short brown hair has thinned out to the point of transparency; his sharp-angled, colorless face is an abstracty bust, its bloodshot eyes, nose, and lips oddly spaced across the surface. Clothes-wise, everything's just a little too fresh off the rack—"casual" stuff with this expensive patina—not to mention that none of it fits properly—strangly Sebadoh T-shirt, massive jeans, which, in his case, reads as hopelessly eggheaded, as opposed to, uh, devil-may-care, or whatever he thinks.

"So . . . uh . . ." Ziggy waves his dad in.

The man hobbles a few feet and throws his suitcase down on the dining-room table, then bends over, clicks open the lid. "First your presents," he says, reaching into the jumble of T-shirts, CD's, socks, uh, what the fuck's *that?* His hands reemerge fists, which he immediately hides in the small of his back. "Pick one."

Ziggy nods toward the left for no particular reason.

Roger's left fist swings around, stops, hovering at chest level, cracks, and this white cloth droops out, looking for all the world like a really huge gob of spit. "I'd like you to slip into this . . ." His remaining fist jabs into view, blooming finger by finger. A small, Pepsi-colored pill bottle is perched on the palm. ". . . then take several of these."

"What *are* they?" Ziggy plucks the bottle, holding it up between him and the ceiling light.

"In my day, we called them *goofballs*. I think you kids use the term *pharmaceutical straitjackets*." Roger lays the spitty cloth, which is actually some sort of, like, silken bikini, over Ziggy's raised arm. "Now, off to the showers." He scrunches his eyes, zigzagging them down Ziggy's chest.

"Okay, cool," Ziggy says. "Ha ha ha."

Roger grins. "It's . . . *spectacular* to see you." He obviously means "see" Ziggy's crotch, though there's nothing of note in that particular region, thanks to the T-shirt, unless his dad's studying his thighs, which *are* totally available, not that Ziggy can imagine them turning guys on, except—oh, yeah, right—in the early days, particularly re: Uncle Ken. Still, they were different back then—short and skinnier, to start with—and, so, probably just, like, cutesy in the way children are to adults right across the board.

"So . . ." Ziggy raises an eyebrow.

"So." Roger glances up. For some reason eye contact sets off this intense, like, commotion, and, by the time Ziggy's brain's back in order, his face is tipped sideways and swirled painfully on his dad's. Their tongues are saliva-wrestling in his mouth. Shit.

Ziggy screws free. "*So* . . . I need to get stoned first,

'cos . . ." He backs away, still shrugging. ". . . uh . . . 'cos
I always do that when I . . . sleep with guys."

Roger reaches behind himself, feels around in the
air until his fingertips scrape the upper edge of the couch.
He sits, whispers, "Whoa," maybe very ironically, and
fans his glistening head. "I haven't been this overwhelmed," he adds, ". . . since I scored with that blond
boy in Ride. Not the short, chunky drummer. The
ethereal one. You know, who writes their material?" He's
studying the air or something over Ziggy's right shoulder,
overly intent, a doctor. "Do you like their music?"

"Yeah, sort of." Ziggy turns, checks his path. Ten,
eleven more steps to the door. "Calhoun's into them."

"Did I ever tell you that delicious little story?"

"I don't think so, uh . . ." Backwards step, backwards step . . .

Roger's eyes focus, relocate, pin Ziggy's. "Hold on
a second. You'll be very amused by this." His slacks have,
like, sprouted this miniature, uh, mountain with a suspiciously hard-on-shaped ridge. "Well, I'd just interviewed
the band, and . . ." He starts fingering the ridge. Shit.
"Darling, *please*. Can't you wait just *one moment?*"

Ziggy halts.

*W*hen Calhoun sleeps, you'd assume he's in some
kind of pain, at first glance anyway. Face stricken, mouth
open, air rustling in and out, thanks to some lingering

asthma. Heroin's just fogged the boy in, made him alter-
nately spacy or tense, and, hence, a rockier emotional
commitment, as psychiatrists might say. But Calhoun's
ambivalence is part of his charm, by his own drugged-out
figuring. Not that he's swimming in friends. Still, Ziggy,
especially, acts so absurdly honored or whatever to know
him, for no particular reason that Calhoun can glean. The
guy's obviously a weird form of addict. Let's leave it at
that. Because Ziggy's real motivations are too complicated to solve when you're zoned this consistently. The
most sincere person on earth can seem so . . . con-
spiratorial, his friendliness such a smoke screen for . . .
something. Insanity? One of heroin's gifts to its users is
how it makes abstract and sort of diffuses anything that's
not an in-relative-focus, quick arm's length away. At the
same time, unfortunately or fortunately, the more allur-
ing the thing, the scarier it reads. And love's about as
ungraspable a thing as is humanly possible, to Calhoun's
way of thinking. Here's his definition. Love: a hybrid
emotion made up of various other emotions collaged by
some weak individual's mind to try to quell a particular
horror that's not been wiped out by more standardized
symbols like Christ, etc. Nietzsche, right? Whatever.
Drugged brains are so easily, pleasantly exhausted. *Whatever*. Luckily or unluckily, Ziggy's love's sort of impossible
to quash. Why? Maybe his frenzy's conducive to Calhoun's dead air, in the same way that people with ultradi-
chotomous astrological signs are supposed to meld thanks
to some hard-to-grasp system of planetary alignment.

Point is, Ziggy's there. And love, however fucked up, is just the beginning of what Calhoun needs these days, even he has to admit. So it's a match. Now, if only . . . If only he'd quit shooting heroin, if only something amazing enough came along to replace it, if only he'd give up peacefulness long enough to search further, if only he'd try a little harder at least. *Please,* kid.

*W*hen the fat man woke up someone chilly and stiff had come to rest on his arm.

Ken flipped his sweaty head, left ear to right.

Robin's face, twisted by bad dreams or something but gorgeous for six, seven seconds, then, blink, blink, a forgettable nothingy object dissolving in Fatso's shock.

"Jesus . . . fucking—" Ken jolted up, yelling.

Ripping open the curtains, a fat man spun 180 degrees, picked his bed out from its surroundings, and, sprawled on top, the most significant-by-default creature he'd ever . . .

A boy like a big piece of chalk.

Ken trudged slowly into the other room.

Tick, tick, tick . . .

He sprinted back.

Fatso sitting by Robin, head cocked, dripping sweat in long, rough strands, like the rays of a horrible sun.

A boy like a board.

The fat man looked half-forlornly at a pale yellow phone on his night table, not thinking anything at first.

Then he wailed toward it.

Behind Ken's immense, sopping back, a Heavy Metal kid cross-faded into . . .

Rrring, rrring, click.

"Frankel," Fatso yelled into the almost-kid-corpse-colored receiver. "You said once . . ." Huge breath in. ". . . didn't you . . ." Huge breath out. ". . . that you'd be interested . . ." Etc. ". . . that you'd pay a lot of money to . . ."

In the telephone's earpiece: "Shi-i-i-it."

Far behind Ken, Robin creaked like a wooden house.

"You could . . ." The fat man gasped. "Do that thing . . . if you hurry."

Robin: Creak.

Earpiece: "Give me a couple of hours."

Click.

Cre-ea-ak.

Don't worry too much about *you-know-what*.

Ken stared out his nightmarish bedroom. In the distance—his kitchen, its table—an outdoorsy light caught something made out of metal or glass, glittering suspiciously.

Ziggy locks himself inside the john, fills a water glass, chases down four or five of the pills Roger brought him. He strips, checks the mirror, not bad, ha ha ha, throws the rubbery curtain aside, and starts a hot, violent shower. "Mm . . ." Revolving under the spray, Ziggy puts himself through the usual scrubbing-down shtick, then, hm, why not, shoves a shampoo-flocked finger way, way up his ass, making sure it's hygienic enough for Mr. Ass Connoisseur or whoever. Spooky. Whoa, he thinks, scrounging around. There's a . . . compartment up there . . . a, like, pocket at the top of the tube that he can't, ouch, travel deep enough into to figure out physically. Remember, he thinks, withdrawing, smelling the finger. "Ugh." Explore that place later. "Don't forget." Then he cracks up for no particular reason. "I'm fucking sto-o-o-oned," he says. He slides purposefully down a tile wall, mock dying, hands crumpled, into the bathtub, which feels like it should be less hard than it is. It's almost impossible to stand, but he gets to his feet with the help of the cowboys-and-Indians-themed shower curtain. He even manages to turn off the spray, stumble onto the mat, defog the mirror temporarily with the wipe of a forearm. "No . . . *way.*" There's a moronic grin stuck to his drippy face. Whoosh, whoosh . . . He can't even towel it off. That's hilarious. Everything's hilarious, until, that is, it's time to put on the pair of costly jockey shorts Roger insisted on giving him. Then he realizes how sloppy he is, and, though he doesn't give a shit at the moment, sloppiness *is* a state he normally avoids at all costs. "Shi-i-i-it." He has to lie down on the floor and yank like a factory worker or something to get the shorts on, they're so tight and difficult to keep hold of for some reason. Clambering to his feet, he squints into the mirror. Oh *duh,* he thinks, seeing the perfect outline of his cock and balls. Every little testicle crevice and cock ridge is visible, as if they were bare, but kind of squished and consistently white. *"No way."* He laughs, flopping back on the toilet seat. "Dad!"

"Yes, dear." Roger's haughty if muffled voice answers so clear it's clear he's been listening outside the door. Yikes.

"I have to, uh . . .," Ziggy says, slurs actually. "Uh, before we do it, I have to . . . call Cricket, this friend of mine. 'Cos . . . I promised."

No reply.

Ziggy grabs onto a towel rack, pulls himself to his feet, weaves through the misty, narrow room, banging against sink, wall, towel rack, etc., unlocks and throws back the door. Roger's sitting cross-legged midhall, naked. "Oh . . . shit." Ziggy shields his eyes. *"God, Dad."*

*I*t wasn't as if I hadn't seen Ziggy's bare chest before, but, sitting there, peering up at that incomparable precipice, I couldn't help but be startled anew by its compact, V-ish configuration—which I could easily call definitive for someone his age—complemented, as planned, by those tight, elegant briefs, through which his splayed genitalia made such a bizarre first impression, like a bagged octopus.

He stood wincing at me, his expression part-dulled by my peacemaking drugs. Yet, as exquisitely hewn as Ziggy was, there remained the distinct if not quite catastrophic downfalls that come with being a teenager, such as how the body's internal organs go temporarily insane—confused by their newfound roominess perhaps—turning formerly nondescript areas, such as the armpits, into gracefully designed exhaust pipes with which others in the world must learn to cope. And Ziggy's pits, with their fine explosions of almost black hair, were, even then, something of a problem, reeking as fiercely as two cornered skunks. Nevertheless, I was determined to read this "problem" in a positive way. For that stink, so generically B.O.-like to the casual sniff, came from *him*.

"Dad, I have to call Cricket." Saying that, Ziggy lurched down the hall, presenting me, thereby, a glorious if staticky view of the ultimate *objet*. It couldn't have been more ideal, at once plump and boy-flat, tenuous as a cloud, with a short, discreet crack—a particular favorite of mine, I might add, since it suggests functionality, period, and, in so doing, indicates the brand of structural perfection one only finds in the minimal.

I leaned back on the wall, entranced, dizzy, as, far away in his bedroom, Ziggy's mildly out-of-control voice started blathering. Eventually I came to my senses, and killed time exploring the house. (More on that later.)

I had reached Brice's room when Ziggy veered through the doorway. He staggered to a central spot, turned his back, gripped his underwear's waistband, and, almost too hastily, propelled the fabric wad to his feet tops. "Freeze," I yelled. Heavens. His was an ass so pale and simple it seemed to be made out of plastic—a blindingly innocent entity, its only discernible flaw the line of frittery hairs in the otherwise invisible crack.

I sat on Brice's futon, rapt, processing that modest little packet of clues for a long time, while Ziggy rocked about, stoned and unsteady. "Now stand up and face me," I said. He did. And there, *there* were his genitals. Decently sized, they leaked, reddish and drab, from a messy brown bush. While the penis is not my particular fetish, this being his, I felt fond of it, even remotely intrigued, etc., as to its agenda.

"Everything okay with your friend?" I managed, hoping a dumb conversation would reroute his steam.

Ziggy nodded. "Yeah," he said. "I sort of set up a three-way for us in two hours. At Cricket's place. That's cool, right? Cricket's a transvestite, but that's no big deal, right?"

"Whatever you like," I replied, smiling warmly. (In truth, his idea only semiintrigued me. I know I should feel a certain kinship with drag queens. Sorry. Still, no doubt this "three-way" would be an opportune time to make a study of him.) "I'm going to retire a few feet," I added, sliding back toward the head board. "You lie face down here." And I patted my former location.

He took his position professionally.

"Talk to me," I said, stroking a babyish asscheek. It immediately tensed into a white boulder.

"What," Ziggy answered.

"How would you characterize this?" I asked, poking the object in various locations. "Say, if you were under oath on a witness stand, and your ass was vital evidence in some murder case."

"What do you *mean?*" Ziggy said, exasperated perhaps, though I heard slight amusement in his tone as well. Remember, I couldn't see his face. "You're so weird."

"Never mind then," I answered. "It's old enough to speak for itself." (Awe had unraveled my wit, which is typical.) I inserted two trembling thumbs in the asscrack and parted it gently, anticipating a noseful of faint, spicy steam. But a strong smell of cloistered shit filled the immediate area, throwing my awe into limbo. For while the nature of an ass more than interests me, my son's interior foulness asked of its scholars an almost inhuman diligence. Still, desire being what it is, I managed to wedge my face into the garrulous crack.

"Dad?" Ziggy's voice queried. It was now approximately five minutes into my worshiping.

"Yes?" I asked back, still faintly nauseous from the stench which my slobbering had only spread farther and more complexly into the room.

"Could you get the Hüsker Dü cassette from the deck in my room and, like, play it in here while we're doing this?" Ziggy gazed over his shoulder at me. Such an extraordinary face, at once pert as a model's and continuously flappable around sputtering blasts of . . . insecurity, I suppose. "Please?"

* * *

*I*n sleep, Calhoun's day reconvenes into an action-packed, disjunctive, misrepresentative trailer of sorts. His sweet, wheezing, pillow-bound face is a theater closed to the public. Ziggy's crashed over here a few times, too depressed and/or stoned to hitch home, watching Calhoun's slack, moonlit expressions change, albeit subtly, along private lines. It's painful for Ziggy to not be right in there with him. But sometimes it's painful, theoretically at least, to be *in there* as well. Like now, when, to nobody's knowledge—not even Calhoun's, since he never remembers his dreams—a blurry image of Ziggy is beating the shit out of him, letting fly with fists, feet, yells, etc., for no stated reason, though Calhoun's dream logic tells him this particular punishment's more than deserved. The fight itself doesn't hurt, but the message is spooky. It makes Calhoun's sleeping face twitch. If he could remember this later, tell Ziggy, perhaps, just perhaps, in a distorted way, he'd be as close to conveying his love as is possible under the terms of his . . . emotional damage? Too bad. He won't recall a detail. It's terrible that friends can't intuit these things from one another, though guessing games keep them together as much as their blab. That's Calhoun's idea, or his big hope at least. He's so lost in this bed. In a perfect world Ziggy would sit beside him, wide awake, shivering with unprocessed tenderness. Calhoun would jolt from the dream, spot his friend, realize everything's cool. They'd lie around bad-mouthing everyone else until . . . whenever, dawn. But Ziggy's so far away and oblivious. The heroin in Calhoun's blood keeps him asleep through it all. Meanwhile, the world's disinterested. When his nightmare ends, Calhoun's face smooths imperceptibly.

*W*hile Roger's gone, Ziggy shakes out his ass doggie style, but saliva keeps trickling out of his crack, down his inner thighs. Footsteps. Click, click . . . click— A frenetic, in-progress guitar solo carves his thoughts into a stupidish mishmash.

"Loud enough?" Roger yells.

. . . *Death's an art, flesh and earth never part* . . .

"Yeah, it's fine, *fine*," Ziggy yells back. Shit. "Just . . . fuck . . . it'll *do!*"

. . . *Spellbound and gagged, I commend your flesh to dirt* . . .

Slayer's Heavy Metal onslaught makes Ziggy's nakedness feel sort of, uh, melodramatic, like if the bedroom was packed with white-trash teen Neanderthals bellowing for him to be fake-sacrificed, which *would* be a hilarious idea, except the music's reminiscent of Robin, whose greenish body's still vomiting, etc., right smackdab in the thick of this sound track too, symbolically at least.

"You have the most symmetrical buttocks I've seen in my life!" Roger yells. "And I've seen quite a number!"

"Thanks!" Ziggy yells back, but he's only heard . . . red or whatever. It's almost like Slayer mixed Roger's monologue in there purposely to illustrate the Satanicesque bullshit they're shrieking about.

. . . *Purged of your dead body, sacrificed of your life* . . .

"Ouch." Ziggy's asscheeks are clutched, wrenched apart. *"Careful."*

. . . *smell the stench of immortality* . . .

There's a whinnying noise from Roger's mouth and/or throat that's so, like, conducive to the Slayer that Ziggy feels ambushed.

. . . *Take my hand and let go of your life* . . .

"Dad!" Ziggy peers over his shoulder, past some unfocused, poppable pimples, to Roger's face, which is sort of poured into his crack, gray and characterless as cement. Crushed underneath, his asshole's being chewed up and buzzed with cold air every couple of seconds.

. . . *At one with the evil that has ruled before* . . .

"This is the wrong cassette!" Ziggy shouts. "Do you mind getting the other one?! It's *inside* the deck! It says *Hüsker Dü* on it!"

Roger surfaces, jowls vibrating, eyes lowered and seemingly wet in respect for . . . Ziggy's symmetry? He looks mentally retarded, but calm, like he's watching some sentimental old film on TV. He unhands Ziggy's ass. It splats shut.

"And please turn this tape off!"

Roger's staggering across the rug.

. . . *Spill your blood and let it run onto—*

Click.

Ziggy si-i-i-its up, way woozy. Roger's so pale, hard to see, and unmuscled, if memory serves, that he's almost a snowman, which would be kind of cool if the thing didn't have an erection.

"Wait," Ziggy slurs.

The snowman stops in the doorway, revolves, frowns at its addressee, one blurred hand pumping away in its crotch.

"We have to, like, stop for a while." Ziggy blinks his eyes clearer. " 'Cos this is freaking me out." He tries to seem serious, which just means engraving some misery mixed with a little hate into his features without actually getting upset. "For a second, okay?"

Roger, who's maybe three-quarters human again, nods. That's better. His fist stops midjerk, loosens, tumbling away from the danger zone. Cool. "Painful associations with Brice?" he says, shutting his eyes.

"Yeah, partly." Ziggy nods in case Roger is peeking. "But also 'cos I'm a total shithead, Dad. I know I am, and . . ." He reaches back, scooping a palmful of bubbly spit from his asscrack. Ugh. ". . . and after sex, people, especially guys, seem to figure that out, whereas, uh, before we have sex there's a thing that . . . makes up for my bad side or something?"

"I'm listening." Roger folds his white arms.

"Let's stop for a few minutes." Ziggy bounces around, making the futon exhale fartily through its buttons. "And, uh . . . we can start up again, like, with

Cricket. Then later on, uh . . . it'll be us by ourselves, and you can do what you want to me. I promise."

Roger sighs, period, so he's definitely pissed. Still, his cock's sluggier every second, and that speaks volumes, at least the kind of volumes Ziggy's interested in.

"Give me a minute to chill," Ziggy says. "So I'll feel more . . . trusting." He's bouncing again. Pfoot, pfoot, pfoot . . . "Like, by myself."

Roger's lips open a fraction. His pointy tongue tip tours them for a couple of seconds. "Mm," he says thoughtfully.

*L*ying next to the Metal corpse, Ken jacked off, constantly adjusting his squint until the thing looked . . . if not quite alive, then appealing.

He'd rolled Robin onto his stomach. Better.

In the fat man's peripheral vision, an unfocused head, back, butt, legs, etc.

It's Ziggy's friend Calhoun, Ken thought. I gave him some very strong heroin. He shot up. He's in dreamland. I get total use of his body. That was the deal. Camera's over there somewhere.

"Shit." Fatso felt around on the floor for his T-shirt, and spread it out over the corpse's un-Calhoun-like head.

Not a peep.

Okay, Ken thought, settling again. Calhoun's in

dreamland. Face unbelievably limp. Probably on his way out. I gave him a fatal dose. Why not? Poor junkie. It's . . . really . . . tragic.

The fat man jacked onwards. With his left hand, he rubbed Robin's stony butt.

So far so perfect.

Calhoun's butt, Ken thought. All clogged up from the dope. Not worth a cent to him. A total hassle, if anything. Never even looked at the fucker for more than a second.

Robin, still totally dead, whether Ken believed it or not.

Maybe the corpse "saw" white light, tunnels, all that.

I've straddled him, Ken thought. Lick his neck, shoulders, back, crack the butt, eat my brains out. Keep glancing up at Calhoun's emptying face to stay emotionally involved.

The fat man raised up on one elbow.

Ken's aerial view of the butt with some Metal kid fuzz at the edges. "Oh, ye-ea-ea-ah."

Robin, the human fridge, full of chilled organs, bones, etc.

I'm fucking Calhoun, Ken thought. Great "bad trip" look in his eyes. Totally tight, clingy asshole. Reach underneath him and fondle his loose dick and balls. Jam my tongue through his jiggling lips.

The fat man really, really jacking off, getting *so damn close*.

Metal corpse, same as it ever was, maybe sturdier.

Calhoun's dead, Ken thought. Happened just a few seconds ago. Check out those eyes. Tell him I hated him so much. That does it. Rear way, way, way back.

The fat man spewed on his belly, shivering, exhaling, and yelling like Hurricane Whoever.

Robin, Ken's ex, going bad about a foot and a half to the left.

Ziggy shuts his bedroom door reasonably tightly considering how Brice's kicks fucked up the lock. He leaps onto his bed, squeak, squeak, listening for Roger's footsteps, but the hall sounds untrammeled. Unfocusing his eyes, he imagines the house is a brothel of sorts, and he's been given a choice of prostitutes between people who look like Nicole and Calhoun. Or . . . better, yeah, he's inside a weird, ultimate brothel that asks which human beings you'd most like to be with, and kidnaps them for you or something. His two beloveds would stand at attention across the room, nude, hands on genitalia, awaiting his verdict. It takes a minute or so to successfully devise likenesses then give them characteristic expressions—perplexed in Calhoun's case, and, uh, well . . . just beautiful in hers. Okay, cool. Weigh the fuckers, ha ha ha. For instance, is her reciprocal lust hotter than Calhoun's complete lack of interest? Whose face would be sexier grinding open-mouthed against his? Which naked body—Cal-

houn's is a sort of deduction since Ziggy's only seen
chunks of the guy (chest, back, arms, legs)—would he go
more insane near? Etc. Vague pluses and minuses are
piling up in vague mental columns. The ideal duo's posing
there, freeze frames. "Can I choose both?" Ziggy sees
himself asking some brothel employee he doesn't even
bother to envision. Sure, break the rules, dude. What a
saint. Thanks. Now Nicole and Calhoun turn in circles like
dazed, avant-garde ballerinas or something. Both bods
are conventionally great in this relaxing, forgettable way.
Hers is just, well, uh . . . he wants to get in there immediately. It's hard to deep-six that idea long enough to give
a thought to Calhoun, but, once Ziggy foregrounds the
guy, backpedals her, there's this different, incredible effect. Like he tears up in seconds. His lips start this "I love
you" mantra that makes stupid tears overflow. Shit. Calhoun, moved, shuffles across the room, sits on the bed
next to Ziggy. After some nervous throat clearing, they
grab and, uh, hug one another, both sobbing like . . .
whatever, children? Ziggy strokes Calhoun's hair, and
vice versa. Tick, tick, tick . . . After a while, Ziggy forces
himself to look up from his best friend's invaluable skin,
etc., and yeah, Nicole's still right there, waiting. He eye-
motions her over. She squeezes between them. Calhoun
shoots him a look of such gratitude, love, excitement, etc.,
that Ziggy has to dig his fingernails into his thighs to keep
from bawling again. At her suggestion, they wedge themselves—boy, girl, boy—lengthwise on the twin bed. Calhoun and he rub, kiss, lick her for minutes. Details don't

matter for some reason. It's ideal, definitely, 'cos he can do what he wants with Nicole, whom he's bonkers about, temporarily at least, and, every once in a while, share some sweet eyeball time with his equally turned-on best friend, whom Nicole's also into. The combination has this peacefulness about it, around which the world of Roger can, like, completely fuck off, explode for all Ziggy cares. And it's during one of these ultrareassuring tête-à-têtes with Calhoun, their cocks snuggling up in her cunt, that, back in the real, horrible world, Ziggy shoots a wad of sperm on his stomach and ribs, gasping so vociferously that it's a miracle Roger's not tiptoeing down the hall, hoping to, like, exploit the situation, but . . . Ziggy listens closely through his bliss, rush, etc. No, the . . . coast's . . . clear.

I spent . . . oh, a half hour touring the living room, hoping to exercise my dormant critical faculties. I think I can say, for the sake of this argument at least, that my ex-boyfriend's taste in furnishings, while primitive, indicated an admirable, obsessive aesthetic of sorts. On a minuscule budget, he'd managed to raise a specific, fine-tuned little world around Ziggy and him—a kind of cut-rate theme-park-in-a-tract-house, referencing the Old West, or should I say the "Old West" as romanticized and muted by Hollywood.

From the Clint Eastwood–esque bent of his videocassettes to the choice of wallpaper, across which a dozen or so violent period scenes—shoot-outs, bronco busting, wagon train attacks, etc.—were faux-carved repeatedly at, say, foot intervals, into a milky brown "bark," the place positively rang with gentrified masculinity. Everywhere I strolled, unkempt boys and unshaven men frolicked in one-dimensional splendor, be they shut up in yellowed, mass-market paperback books, reduced and frozen in tasteless porcelain figurines, or made heroically fluorescent via the worst paintings one could imagine.

There was a very brief phase in rock music's development, around the early eighties if memory serves, when punk rock's growing pains found a few rather lesser practitioners infusing their fierce, three-chord tunes with a slight countryish swagger, as if this historical referent would somehow legitimize their highly unpopular music. Cowpunk, as this subgenre came to be known, was a rickety concoction at best, but it reads interestingly in retrospect, if, that is, one approaches rock music as a kind of psychological graph of its particular artists. I subscribe to this reading, of course. And it seemed a logical leap to apply this same critical stance to the "art" of Brice McCauley, interior designer.

In Westerns, Brice undoubtedly believed he'd unearthed an official, historical grounding of sorts for his lack of morality. Were he back in Laredo, Dodge City, or any one of those mythical hamlets, there'd have been, to his thinking, a general consensus about the necessity of cruelty. Presumably wife beating, child abuse, rape—

these contemporary no-nos were just part and parcel of preindustrialized life. Brutalized children blossomed happily into renowned brutalizers, unself-consciously getting their rocks off, oblivious to the now ingrained, rather Big Brother–ish lessons of psychoanalysis. Safe in his dim re-creation of a lawless utopia, Brice could lord his foul moods over Ziggy, et al., and come away both with a stuntmanlike rush *and* the self-respect of a dedicated Revisionist. Fascinating.

*T*he fat man exhaled into the telephone's mouthpiece, creating a tinny whirlwind in his listening ear.

"Hello," said a sleepy voice.

"Calhoun?" Ken closed his eyes, wobbly dick squashed to shit in one fist, skinny blond baby-faced junkie kid snagged in his head.

"Yeah, who's this?"

"Ziggy's uncle." In Ken's head, Calhoun sat on his lap, shooting up, jeans unzipped, too high to give a shit. "I met you once when—"

"What do you want?"

"Some mutual back scratching." Ken slid down low in the couch, jacking off. Calhoun's deep, edgy voice helped the situation immensely.

"I was asleep."

Hard to keep the old voice steady. "Ziggy says . . . you have a heroin problem . . . I know what that can do . . . to one's finances . . . Maybe I could help you out with some . . . money, say . . . three hundred dollars . . . in return for . . . a sexual favor."

"I'm not gay."

"I know." In Ken's head, Calhoun slumped forward, nodding, face eerily *gone*. "What I'm proposing's . . . a simple trade-off . . . You're paid, I get . . . quality time with your body." Ken was mentally helping Calhoun to the Sex Hole. "You don't have to . . . touch me. You . . . don't have to look at me . . . Get as high as you . . . want. Pretend I'm not . . . there."

"Jesus."

Calhoun's scarecrowlike body facedown on a sharply lit bed. "Let's say *four* hundred dollars."

"Nope."

"I can score you some . . . really good heroin." Pump, pump, pump . . . "A friend of mine . . . sells the purest dope . . . in the city." In secret, Ken slapped, ate, slugged, fucked Calhoun's flat, clogged-up butt.

"Hm. Is it in rock form or powder?"

"Whichever you like." Under Ken's eyelids, Calhoun was gradually O.D.'ing where nobody knew who could give a shit.

Calhoun didn't talk for a moment. "You know, you're disgusting."

In Ken's mind, Calhoun's big mouth started rattling. Pump, pump, pump . . . "So keep your eyes shut." He felt *incredibly close*.

"Fuck off." The phone clicked.

Ken exploded in Calhoun's corpse. "Oh, ye-ea-ea-

ah," he said, dripping two strings of sperm on his gigantic
stomach.

In the fat man's ear, a tinny whirlwind.

$\mathbf{Z}$iggy's organized his bed into a shambly office.
Short stack of fresh paper, several petrified copies of *Spin*
magazine to keep the paper from buckling, pencil, artist's
eraser, a warped pile of recent *I Apologize* drawings and
interviews. He's even uprighted the Polaroid of Calhoun
and him, sort of for the same basic reason that business
types fill up their offices with shots of loyal family mem-
bers. Cool. Ziggy, gulp, lifts the black telephone onto his
"desk," quickly dialing a number so magic, to his mind,
it could be the combination to some safe where, uh,
Hüsker Dü is imprisoned or something.

Click.

"Yeah, what?"

"Oh, shit. Were you asleep?" Ziggy's performing a
sort of baton twirl–type thing with his pencil. "My sense
of time's a mess. Sorry."

"I wish." Calhoun exhales.

"But I was calling to interview you for my magazine. And you're probably too wrecked right now,
so . . . " Ziggy reaches behind him and slides Hüsker Dü's
Zen Arcade into the tape deck. It blasts on. He turns it
down.

"That's okay." Calhoun's obviously lighting a cigarette, so maybe it *is*, like, okay. "What do you want to . . . ? Wait." His lighter scratch-scratches. "So . . . I get kind of belligerent in interviews."

Ziggy writes Calhoun's first name across the top of the page in huge letters. "When were you interviewed before?"

"For jobs. *You* know."

"Well, this'll be cooler than that, I hope, ha ha ha." Ziggy finishes writing the *N*.

"It'd have to be."

"Yeah." Ziggy's still laughing. "So, uh, let me start with some background. You've probably told me before, but say it again for the record. Slowly, 'cos I'm copying everything down. Uh . . . do you consider yourself a, like, victim of sexual abuse, or just of abuse in general? When you were a kid, I mean."

Calhoun chuckles. "Hm."

"Wasn't your mother an alcoholic or something?"

"Sort of, but . . . is *that* what you mean?"

Ziggy's transcribing. "Well, it fucked you up."

"I guess," Calhoun says. "But my mom's all right." He takes a drag. "I think that, mm . . . 'substance abuse' runs in my family. So I understand her side of things, and she'll probably understand mine, if I tell her."

"Well, you're obviously a great person. So she didn't really ruin you *too* much."

Calhoun snorts. "Thanks."

"Yeah, no problem." Ziggy laughs nervously. "Wait a second, I'm . . . writing . . . Okay, cool."

"So I decided to quit." Calhoun takes a drag, probably waiting for Ziggy to ask him, "Quit what?" But by the time Ziggy gets it, Calhoun adds, "Quit heroin."

"*Really?* When?" Ziggy writes "Calhoun quits" in block letters.

"Today. I'm gonna take my last shot in a minute."

"God, that's *great*. But . . . Why, or . . . ?"

"Because it's fucking me up. I can't write. My arms . . . are just dead. I have to shoot in my hands, and they're swollen." Calhoun clears his throat. "I look . . . deformed."

"I'll come stay with you while you're quitting." Ziggy throws down the pencil. " 'Cos I hear it's pretty hard. I can, like, get your cigarettes and cook you food and stuff. If that's cool."

"If you want to. But . . . you have to leave me alone if—"

"No problem. I'll just . . . work on my magazine or something. *God*, Calhoun. That's . . . I love you *so much*, and . . . yeah, it's been scary to see you . . . subdued. Is that the right word? I mean, you're always, *always* amazing to be around, but . . . Well, you'll be happier, right?"

Calhoun chuckles. "I don't know about that. But at least I'll have orgasms. See, when you're on heroin, sex isn't . . . mm, a priority."

"I heard," Ziggy says. "Sounds kind of, uh . . . peaceful, ha ha. 'Cos sex just ruins everything. Look where it's gotten me."

"Yeah."

"I guess if I could have sex with somebody I loved . . . Well, I sort of love Roger. *Maybe.* And Nicole's okay, but . . ." Ziggy reaches over and plucks the Polaroid of Calhoun and him from the night table. "Anyway, the person I really, really love is, like, a straight guy, so . . . so . . ." He smiles at the image. *"Thanks a lot, pal."* That's just a joke, but, realizing what he actually said and to whom, Ziggy slams the receiver against his ear.

"Jesus . . . ," Calhoun says. "Is that something you think about a lot?"

"About us sleeping together?" Ziggy holds the Polaroid close to his face, and squints into his best friend's eyes. They're greenish blue specks with teensy-weensy black bull's-eyes.

"Yeah." Calhoun takes a drag.

"No, no, no." Ziggy checks out his own little eyes, which are blissed like an infant's. "It's just, uh, weird that I find, like, the person I most care about in the world, not sexually or anything, and you're straight. Maybe that's how it's supposed to be, though."

"So you've decided you're gay?" Calhoun takes a drag.

"No, uh . . . Shit." Ziggy tosses the Polaroid away, digs a hand in his hair, concentrates. "Never mind. I'm just blabbing. I'm still whatever I always was. Bisexual, I guess."

"I think it's better this way," Calhoun says.

"I agree." Ziggy feels like he's going to cry. So he yanks his haircut into loonyville. "It's kind of, uh . . . refreshing, ha ha ha." He twiddles the hair.

"I hope it's okay with you."

"It's *definitely* okay with me." Ziggy's lower lip's going crazy for whatever reason.

"Good."

"Yeah," Ziggy says. "What about the idea, though, of, like, us both, uh . . . fucking a girl at the same time? Is that . . . interesting at all? 'Cos . . . Shit, *I* don't know. Maybe that'd be, like, a compromise."

Calhoun clears his throat. "But wouldn't you . . . I know this sounds presumptuous . . . wouldn't you want to do more things to me than to her? I mean, since you feel the way you do about me?"

"No, no, uh—"

"I'm just not interested in men at all."

"Yeah, I know."

"And I think I'm more of a one-on-one type of person."

"Yeah, yeah. That's cool. Really, though, it's not about fucking you. It's . . . like . . . we're brothers?"

There's a stretch of Calhoun's patented, nerve-rack-ing silence. "So . . . ," he says. "How's it going with your father?"

"Oh, uh . . . *horrible.*" Ziggy lowers his voice. "We used to talk about bands and drive around . . . it was great, but now he's pressuring me to have sex *every second.* He's just, like, this total fucking sleazeball. I don't know *what* I was *thinking.*" Ziggy pounds his forehead. Again, again.

"Come on over," says Calhoun. "Now. Blow him off."

"Yeah, I will. In a while. But I promised the guy,

and, uh, I sort of have to go through with it. I'll be there tonight, though, for sure, and . . . Can I crash at your place for a few days?"

"Sure, but . . . don't get any funny ideas." Calhoun chuckles. "Sorry. And bring along that heroin you bought, if you have any left. In case I can't quit. Then I won't have to score when I'm sick."

"Okay," Ziggy says, feeling his pocket to make sure it's still in there. Yeah. "Will do."

"See ya later."

"Oh, wait." Ziggy grabs the pencil, paper. "My interview, uh . . ."

"Can't we do it tonight? I'm kind of beat."

"No problem. That's probably better anyway. 'Cos then I'll be looking at your face, ha ha ha."

"Yeah," says Calhoun.

"And . . . *shit*, I'm so glad you're gonna quit heroin." Ziggy draws a big box around the words "Calhoun quits."

"I'll do my best." Calhoun lets out or takes in a scared-sounding drag.

"And . . . forgive me, okay?" Ziggy's doodling the box into a kind of, like, punk picture frame. "For, uh, being so emotional with you."

"Yeah, sure."

"I . . ." Ziggy really wants to convey how he feels, though he's so unsure what that entails that his mouth's stuck just sorting it out. Doodle, doodle. "Uh . . . oh, fuck . . . I'm . . ."

"Don't worry about it," says Calhoun immediately.

"No, it's just . . . that, uh . . . Fuck, fuck, fuck. Do you know what I'm going to say?"

Calhoun takes a drag.

"Should I say it or not?" Ziggy squints at the punk picture frame, which looks just realistic enough that it's worth, like, refining a little.

"It's up to you."

"But would it help you to know how I feel?" Doodle, doodle.

"I know how you feel."

"And . . . well, does it bother you, or . . . ?"

"Nope." Calhoun clears his throat.

"Shit, uh . . . Okay then, can I ask you the worst question I'll ever ask you, and just get it over with now, if I promise to never ever mention it again?" Ziggy's started decorating the frame with minuscule, screaming human faces.

Calhoun takes a drag.

"Uh, do you love me? I don't mean are you in love with me, 'cos I know you're not, and I'm not in love with you either, don't worry. I mean 'love,' you know?"

"Yeah."

"Are you just saying that so I'll shut up?"

Calhoun chuckles. "Of course."

"So," Ziggy tries to say, but the word's all, like, shredded. He has to shake his head to keep from bawling this second. "That's . . ."

"No, I'm lying." Calhoun breathes out. "Look, I don't know what love means. I really like you a lot. Maybe I love you, *I* don't know."

"You're the greatest person in the world."

"*Jesus*, Ziggy." Calhoun starts scratch-scratching his lighter, it sounds like.

"I believe that," Ziggy says. "And I just feel incredibly lucky to know you. Every second of knowing you has been . . . Wait . . ." Tears are rolling. "Sorry . . ." He sobs. "Shit, you just . . ." He jags the mouthpiece about a foot from his mouth.

"Thanks," says Calhoun's voice. It's far off.

Ziggy slaps one hand over his wet, shaky face to keep the noise down so Roger won't hear him, rush in, and ruin everything.

"Come on over." Calhoun takes a drag.

"I . . . can't." Ziggy sniffles. "Uh, but tonight."

"Look, you can come to my place or call me *anytime you want*, okay?"

Ziggy's throat squeaks involuntarily.

"You . . . you're my best friend. Hm . . . Look, we can talk all this shit out tonight."

Ziggy nods, squeaks.

"You're definitely going to come."

Ziggy forces the pencil to page and draws a screaming face. "Yeah."

"Okay." Calhoun takes a drag. "See ya later then. I . . . have to go."

Click.

* * *

*C*alhoun's staring at an incompetent painting of
Paris. What . . . has . . . he . . . done? On the one hand,
he meant whatever he just said to Ziggy, even if the whole
conversation's already a wreck in his memory. Compas-
sion burst of out of his mouth on its own. At the same
time, no words have ever definitively caught what he
means. So every time he speaks up he's a liar in some
sense. Calhoun has relatively successfully danced—
though it's more like a veer—around his emotions for
years, it seems. Partially that's to protect other people. In
any case, he's become an enigma, even to himself, though
there's a handful of relatives who'd more than love to
debunk his philosophy and prove how conventionally
fucked up he is. To them, he's a scared, irresponsible,
obnoxious, perpetual child whose life-style constitutes a
simplistic disloyalty. And they're waiting for him to ac-
custom himself to his fate—membership in their incestu-
ous, small-town kingdom, i.e., a handful of drunks and
control freaks for whom a distorted, shrunken world's
better than facing the real one. They've made him distrust
people. And he's tried very hard to be comfortable alone,
with heroin's help. But Ziggy's friendship is fucking
things up now, because the guy's so okay if insistent and
needy. Ziggy's a golden, complicated opportunity to
. . . whatever, feel stuff without mentally strangling it at
conception. Still, who's to say the guy won't get bored
with mere friendliness, chase down the next basket case he

can find, leaving Calhoun with all variety of painfully dug up emotion and nowhere to aim it, except maybe into his novel, one paragraph of which is still barely visible across his room in the laptop's small, windswept blue window? Like . . . decrepit skywriting? Calhoun blinks himself to attention, strolls over, rereads it. Tick, tick, tick . . . Not bad. His description of Gwen, meaning Josie, is strangely . . . what? Sad but riveting, and kind of distantly sexy too. Thanks to him—or, more specifically, thanks to his heroin "problem"—she's found her way into the ominous rest of the world. She's probably over. Gwen's still "around." Heroin's going away maybe. He's practically alone, as he wished. Ziggy cares, for whatever that's worth. The cursor pulsates hypnotically. Tick, tick, tick . . .

Mr. Frankel, a slight, balding, neatly dressed man in his late forties, entered Ken's bedroom a foot and a half behind his lumbering host. Nervous little baby stepettes.

"So . . ." Ken's shrug indicated the corpse, not that anybody could've overlooked it.

One dusty window's glow over everything.

"You can tell. Right away." Frankel leaned over the soon-to-rot kid, one fingertip holding his glasses in place.

"Mm-hm."

A delicate, stub-fingered hand pressing down on a chest like a crushed, shrink-wrapped cage.

"What a perfect temperature," said Frankel. His palm touched the genitals. Icy. "Oh my God." He pushed down. Harder. Goose bumps swallowed that arm.

"You want to see him alive?"

Tick, tick, tick . . .

Back in the living room, Fatso pushed PLAY. "First the buildup," he said. "Getting to know Robin."

On TV, Robin, casually dressed, hair intact, sto-o-oned, slouched on a tartan couch, smirking.

Frankel, rapt, kneeling close to the TV. "You're a fortunate man." He eyed Ken.

Ken pushed SLOW MOTION.

Frankel, back on his feet, hands in pants pockets, walking in very crude circles.

On TV, Robin's face looking totally abstract.

The past. FAST FORWARD, PLAY.

On TV, same kid, naked, zonked on a bed, really sparkly, being slowly reduced to a narrow white stripe under Fatso here.

Two tight-lipped men staring into a TV set, faces gone . . . religioso, eyes and mouths in particular.

No sound.

"Details," said Frankel.

The fat man pushed FAST FORWARD. "How so?" PLAY.

"Anything at all."

On TV, same kid with his head shaved, gagged, arms and legs flung in the air, overly lit into an eggshell white splash.

Frankel walked into Ken's bedroom, glancing back at the TV, peering into the room, TV, room, TV, room . . .

"Well, he was a big Heavy Metal fan." Ken pushed PAUSE.

. . . TV, room . . .

"Thirteen years old."

. . . TV, room . . .

On TV, a freeze-frame of Robin not that far removed from the corpse over there.

"And that's about all . . . I—"

"Ready," said Frankel, basically to himself. He took a baby step backwards.

PLAY.

On TV, same kid, face unbelievably slutty, whether he'd planned it or not.

In the world, a door creaking shut.

Ziggy, still a bit puffy-eyed and sniffling, sits, or, rather, bounces shotgun in Roger's red Honda Civic, suburbia smeared to either side. "Dad?" Ziggy eyeballs the guy, who's changed his clothes to look even more teen-ager-friendly, though it just makes him seem like a kid with a really bad body and face. "I'm sorry I was on the phone for so long, but I decided some important, uh . . . stuff, you know?" The car jolts into its next highest gear. "About me and Calhoun. You know, my best friend." Roger's fists knot, empurple on the steering wheel. "No, *listen*," Ziggy says, waving his arms around. "I got upset with him, and I never do that, 'cos he, like, hates it. But he acted incredibly nice. And, uh . . . I guess I realized . . . what?" Ziggy pounds on his forehead. ". . . that Calhoun needs his friends to, like, be really insane before . . . Shit, I can't explain it. But he *trusts* me now, that's the thing. It's *so amazing.*" Ziggy grins hugely at everything. "And I never trust anyone either. So it's like . . . I've been testing him too. And, you know, I guess he passed, 'cos he . . . *sort of* said he *loved* me. *Just now.*" Ziggy turns his happiness on Roger, who's blanked out, eyes fixed on the road, not listening, though that's obviously impossible, because of . . . physics or whatever. Shit. "Anyway, you don't care. Fuck it." Ziggy glares out the side window, chewing his bottom lip. House, house, house, house . . . indistinguishably blurred. "Take a right here," he mumbles. The car's turned so suddenly that Ziggy grabs onto the dashboard, and just avoids falling face first into Roger's lap, which, uh, was probably the secret plan, knowing his dad. "It's, like, three blocks up there on the right," Ziggy adds, resettling. He presses his face to the glass. Roger floors it. "And, uh . . . I'm also not sure anymore about moving to New York with you." . . . house, house, house . . . " 'Cos Calhoun *needs* me. He's quitting heroin, and I'm going to help him or whatever, so . . ." Deep in the exterior blur, a plaque, reflective white, numbered 832. Ziggy points. "Oh, *there. Stop!*" he yells. They've just whizzed by a house with nothing particularly noteworthy about it, except for how manicured to death the front yard is. *"Back there."* Scre-e-e-e-ech.

*W*hen Calhoun nods, if he's lucky, it's something like watching cartoons through the wrong end of a telescope. Well, not exactly *cartoons*. The hallucinations seem real, but the content's ridiculous. They're like loops of little snips from uninteresting movies he's zoned out in front of. Delicate, meaningless moments that start out as tiny as dots, then rocket toward him down a fuzzily defined, grayish funnel, only to disintegrate on contact with . . . the tip of Calhoun's nose or whatever. Eyes shut, mouth hanging open, he looks sort of mentally handicapped. Or he might look that way to a stranger . . . somebody who didn't give a shit about him. To Ziggy et al., he looks like he's dead. Truth is, he's never been happier. The dichotomy's insane. Heroin is so sophisticated it's evil. Or if evil exists, heroin must be its chief go-between. How does one tell somebody this fucking peaceful to give it up, that he has to go back to functioning properly in one's conception of the appropriate world? It doesn't make sense. Ziggy just winds up praying in private like Calhoun is God, feeling helpless and too idealistic. Because . . . What could he say? Calhoun, your incapacitation is frightening me, or . . . If you O.D., I'll be completely destroyed, meanwhile crossing his fingers in hopes his well-being still counts for anything with the guy. It does and it doesn't. Certainly Calhoun can't tell him so. Luckily, Ziggy's half-learned how to sidestep his friend's generalized behavior, decode contracted eyes, sift through that fuzz, overvalue the warmth of their rare outbound flickers. They've become the most beautiful things in the world, like the muffled cries of hikers trapped in landslides in the middle of nowhere. He's learned to let them spark his imagination. Still, pray and daydream as Ziggy might, he can't quite reconfigure what's here. Here: a skinny blond teenager pickled in heroin, slack-faced, fallen limp as a corpse, brain discarding his lovers and friends for a half-life in decorous seclusion, unconcerned how it looks, or who he's upset along the way, figuring nobody else will ever wander this far, check.

Ken sat absorbing the Robin porn videotape, especially its earliest, fully clothed, softer-core part for some reason.

Perfect kid.

Yow.

In the fat man's mind: This is my finest . . .

Robin, guffawing, head bobbing, hair flying in tempo with . . . what's-their-name, that Heavy Metal band he loved so much, and . . . just . . . *man oh man*, just an edible-beyond-belief kid, if, that is, you don't know he's about to O.D. in a few hours. Or . . .

A painfully hardening bump in the crotch of Ken's pants.

Not . . . *again*.

In the fat man's mind: Or . . . maybe knowing that Robin is dead makes this tape more profound just as long as you don't have to look at his corpse, or . . .

Metal kid's face zooming in, out, in, out.

Perfect "know-it-all" eyes.

Ken fingered his bump bigger.

In the fat man's mind: Or . . . shoot some footage of Robin's dead body and edit it onto the end of the tape to give this emotional weight and to jack the price skyward, or . . .

Ken fast-forwarded through some head banging and so on until he saw skin.

Play.

Robin, nude, dru-u-u-unk, pinching his nipples goofily on the fold-out bed.

Perfect ironic-yet-vulnerable expression.

Ken whipped it out.

Pump, pump, pump . . .

"Show . . . me . . . your . . . butt . . . kid."

Metal kid rising magically to his knees, turning, and sort of shoving that thing toward the camera until it gets blurred beyond all recognition.

An Orson Welles–type seeing God in an unfocused butt shot.

Pump, pump, pump . . .

In the fat man's mind: Or . . . keep the kid's corpse around and shoot its decomposition then market the whole Robin tape and get infamous in certain circles, or . . .

Perfect plan.

Pump, pump—
"Yo-o-ow."
Ken dropped a bit of sperm on his stomach *again*.
Again.

Ziggy, Cricket, and Roger are boozing it up in
his/her parents' dull living room. Really, the place barely
registers, to Ziggy at least. Cricket's prone on the carpet,
cross-eyed, trying to braid the blondish hairs in one wide
open armpit. Roger holds court on a couch, having
dragged Ziggy—who's an oversized Raggedy Andy doll,
period—into his lap. The man's imitating a, like, auction-
eer, his usual haughty voice smeared by vodka tonics and
all twisted up by his role. "What am I bid?" he warbles
hectically. "For this . . . god?"

"Oh, fuck you," Ziggy slurs, not thinking anything.
He waves his beer around.

"Googolplex dollars," Cricket mumbles, still
braiding.

"Oh my *God*, ladies and *gentlemen*. We have a *tie*
between the bidder in . . . a badly fitting blue housedress,
and the bidder in . . ." Roger tilts Ziggy forward by the
scruff of the neck, presumably to check his own outfit.
". . . in stone-washed blue jeans and a My Bloody Valentine T-shirt."

"Fu-u-ck yo-o-ou," Ziggy bellows.

Cricket squeaks agreeably.

"Let's go somewhere . . . else," Roger continues. He's started to sort of, like, frisk Ziggy's . . . groin for the most part. ". . . and divide up our loot, mm?"

Cricket frees the braid. It immediately unties itself, droops. *"I* know where," he/she mumbles, eyes locked on that pit, its hairs, which drunkenness must've redesigned into something mysterious like, uh, a dancing flame? Blink.

Ziggy, belted by Roger's arms, weaves on tiptoe through the living room's beige and/or brown furniture, almost destroying a couple of items en route, heading in the direction of Cricket's ass, which, as the boy/girl sashays away, restyles the back of his/her dress into an almost great artwork, by Ziggy's temporarily questionable standards. He/she keeps twisting around, smiling sexily over his/her shoulder. Or . . . maybe he/she's smirking at Ziggy's inebriated condition. Either way, he doesn't fucking care anymore. They've wound up in a small, blurry room whose walls are, like, collaged floor to ceiling with pictures of some cute young guy, shot at numerous ages, in various attire, hair at all different lengths, always sporting the same smarmy look on his face, like he's been trying to get you in bed all his life or whatever, even though he's, like, fourteen at the oldest. Ziggy's flung on a mattress, bounce, bounce. Roger half-tickles, half-strips him, growling comedically. To Ziggy's general right, a kind of Cricket hologram floats around, giggling at them. Occasionally he/she/it removes a wispy article of clothing.

Watching the dress descend his/her/its pale, saggy chest gets Ziggy . . . if not quite hard, then tingly where sex hibernates. "Cricket," he whispers, about the time the expensive shorts scratch past his ankles.

"Ziggy," the boy/girl/hologram echoes back, maybe sort of ironically.

Roger shakes hands or whatever with Ziggy's cock, balls. Loving that, eyeing Cricket's much-bigger-than-normal-boys' nipples, Ziggy forces himself to sit up, or almost. "That's *all*, Dad." He slaps Roger's wrist, and collapses back onto the top sheet. "It's great, but don't do anything weirder yet, okay?"

Cricket, completely nude, yeah, walks around the room's perimeter, studying smarmy guy pictures. He/she has a babyish, almost-girl bod that's nearly blown by his/her huge, jelly-colored genitalia. Luckily drunkenness, transvestism . . . something, has smudged their details into this kind of interesting scar.

"Over *here*," Ziggy says, pounding once near his hip. "Oh, gre-ea-ea-at." Roger's just licked his cock. "Ha ha ha . . . thanks, Dad." Again. The sensation's indescribable, like however the opposite of being tortured to death might feel. So he zones into fantasy—Dad, Cricket, him mashed simplistically together. Tick, tick . . .

When Ziggy refocuses ten, maybe twelve seconds later, Cricket's right there—we're talking inches away—doubled over his hips, more specifically the crotch, studying Roger's blow job like he/she's a . . . whatchacallit

. . . paramedic, but less scary obviously, his/her mascaraed eyes back in their flame-watching, hypnotized mode. "So, uh . . . what're you thinking about, Cricket?"

"I don't know," he/she says quietly. "It's kind of new to me."

"A real . . . mixed . . . blessing . . . no?" Roger says, slurping away. "But . . . hold on." He leans back and T-shirts his mouth dry, then sneaks a fingertip underneath Ziggy's balls, flipping them back, and, with his other hand, hoisting up one of the boy's useless legs, to improve Cricket's view of . . . the asshole presumably. "Feast your eyes."

"Yeah, feast," Ziggy says, trying to add some tour-guide-esque firmness to his sprawled, uncooperative voice. ". . . on the . . . the . . . uh, most famous . . . uh . . ." He squints at his dad. ". . . uh . . ."

"The Hope diamond of assholes," Roger says evenly.

"Ha ha ha, yeah." Ziggy pans his squint over to Cricket, who looks . . . uh . . . hard to tell.

"The little asshole that could," Roger says.

"Totally!" Ziggy guffaws. The world blurs for a second.

"The asshole that cured cancer."

"Yeah, but . . ." Ziggy's suddenly confused. He raises his head. "Cancer's not cured, or . . . is it?"

Roger and Cricket are grinning at him with identical weirdness.

"I have this splendid idea." Roger leans over and whispers a word or two to his accomplice.

"Wait!" Cricket shuts his/her eyes. The scribbled-on lids quake a few times. "Okay, what's rimming like?"

Ziggy can't fucking believe this. "For me or for Dad?" he slurs.

"For Dad, I guess." Cricket jabs a thumb at Roger.

"Depends," Roger says. "On how you feel about Ziggy. Since he's my son, and, concurrently, my type, there's no small significance in the activity. Boys' asses are just about the most imperious objects on earth, trust me. But they *do* smell like asses. That's an acquired taste, certainly. And Ziggy's only human, dear, much as you and I may find that difficult to accept. So, if you're asking me for a recommendation, I say, Yes, proceed. Only don't expect miracles."

Cricket nods stiffly. "And it feels good, Ziggy?"

"Oh, *wow,*" he says—gushes might be more accurate. Roger's started tickling his asshole, which, in and of itself, is just forgettably nice, but the sensation's kind of filtering into his . . . cavern, where it completely transcends the term *genius.* "That feels . . . amazing, Dad. Uh . . . but, uh . . . it's up to you, Cricket. If you don't want to I . . . understand."

Cricket hugs his/herself. "I could try."

Roger's finger, ouch, plunges. "Unh . . . *fuck,*" Ziggy squawks. "I mean . . . thanks, Cricket. I . . . love you." He sort of does maybe.

"And now . . . ," Roger says. ". . . prepare your-self . . ." The finger's yanked. *Ouch.* ". . . for a shock." Resting Ziggy's aloft, numbed-out leg against his My Bloody Valentine T-shirt, Roger reaches for you-know-where, hands crumpled and trembling like stranglers' in bad TV movies. They wad Ziggy's cheeks, then jolt in opposite directions. "Riveting, isn't it?"

"It's . . . impressive." Cricket cocks an eyebrow at Ziggy. "It *is.*"

"Kneel here in front of me," Roger says. He releases the asshole, pfoot, letting go of the leg, flop, squeak, squeak. "Roll over, Ziggy," he adds, then straightens his posture and holds out both arms. Giggling, Cricket sits in this "chair." He/she settles back into the flabby uphol-stery. Ziggy rolls over, which isn't that easy to do, but . . . "Put your head *here,* dear." The man paws through Cricket's hair, pinching his/her earlobes. ". . . right . . . in line . . . with the . . . *object.*" He's tugging his/her embarrassed face down, down . . . "There."

Ziggy's been watching them over his shoulder, espe-cially Cricket, whose lips and nose are contorting an inch from his ass, maybe like someone deciding to drink or not to drink from a rusty water fountain. Shit. So Ziggy flat-tens, and closes his eyes to, like, protect what he has of a hard-on.

"Golly," says Cricket's voice. "It doesn't smell *so* bad."

Ziggy's too drunk, relieved, horny, etc., to thank

him/her properly. "God," he blurts, figuring no other word has more clout, meaning-wise.

"Dive in," urges Roger's voice.

Ziggy closes his eyes. Breaths are rustling his ass hairs. Whoosh . . . whoosh . . . His cock's grown as hard as superhumanly possible. Tick, tick, tick . . . Hm . . . tick, tick . . . When he raises up, checks to see what's the delay, Roger's breathing in Cricket's old spot, and he/she's seated cross-legged to Ziggy's left, slumped way over, head in hands, face all smushed around the fingers. "What . . . uh . . . happened?"

"Our friend couldn't handle the . . . aroma, let's say." Roger grins at Ziggy's ass conspiratorially.

Cricket clears his/her throat.

"That's okay." Ziggy squints, trying to find Cricket's eyes in that crosshatch of skin, knuckles, fingernails, makeup. "Rimming's my dad's thing. I don't care about it. But, uh—"

"Quick, dears," says Roger's voice. Ziggy's right asscheek is bitten, tugged up in the air, shaken roughly, and freed. Ouch. "Before we lose our momentum."

Cricket nods and falls backwards. He/she raises, folds, shifts his/her shaved legs around until they're just stubbly white piles on his/her chest, with two feet sticking out of them. "Like this?" he/she asks, licking a couple of fingers. "The only other . . . time I did it . . . it happened . . . like this." The wet fingers smear all inside his/her asscrack.

"Yeah, that's cool," Ziggy says. He's trying to adjust to the fact that his/her ass is an ass, period, and not anything intimidating like a vagina. "You look, uh . . . hot." That sounded wrong. "Sorry." He rises unsteadily to his hands and knees, crawls to the edge of Cricket's bed, scanning the floor for his clothes. Roger's folded, stacked them in a For Sale–type pile. Ziggy topples it, scrounging around in the ruins until he locates the pint-sized accordion of condom packs. Ripping one free, he peels off the wrapper, unrolls a milky balloon down his hard-on, turns, and, averting his eyes, guides it into Cricket's ass. Luckily, he/she's preoccupied elsewhere, eyes locked on . . . the cute young guy wallpaper? Poke, poke . . . Something gives. "Whoa, *hey*." He gasps. "You're so . . . tight. Sorry." He/she nods stiffly. Cold hands, Roger's obviously, scrunch and spread Ziggy's asscheeks. Ouch. "Hey, don't . . ." Oh, *who cares?* A face like a packaged-up boulder starts rolling around back there. It's . . . mildly entertaining. Cool. Ziggy jabs, jabs, jabs, jabs, etc., into Cricket's hole, stoned on its heat, eyes shut, rerunning that scene with Nicole from the other night, albeit slightly improved on in parts. Tick, tick . . . Jab, jab— *"Fuck."* Ziggy's accidentally come. Sperm's lobbing into the condom's bunched nipple. "Shi-i-it." Almost the second he runs out, Ziggy starts feeling . . . well, depressed about covers it. That snowballs. "No, *please*," he whispers. "N-n-not . . ." Roger's face is so far up his ass, it's like the guy wants to leave some sort of permanent impression, maybe so he can slip in more easily next time. Fair enough, but, for whatever reason, it makes Ziggy burst into tears. Shit.

"Fash-shin-nat-ting," says a muffled Roger.

"Are you . . . *okay*, Ziggy?" Cricket asks. He/she's raised up on his/her elbows. Deep in those too made-up eyes, there's this glimmer of kindness or something he can't quite make out.

"I . . . I . . . d-don't know . . . why . . . this happens," Ziggy says, slugging his chest.

"If there's anything I can—"

"Hey, quit!" Ziggy twists around, slugs Roger's head. "Fuck, you're pissing me off!" Again, again. The guy doesn't budge. Maybe he's stuck there or something. "If you loved me . . ."—Ziggy slugs—". . . you wouldn't *rim* me while I'm *crying.*" This time he hits Roger's head so violently it's knocked loose. "That's the *truth,* you . . . *scum!*" Through Ziggy's tears, something, a glittering outline, presumably Roger's, squeak, squeak, squeak, leaves the bed. "Fucking scum!" The figure wobbles off. "Die you *fuck!*"

*C*alhoun's having a dream that he'll never remember. Josie's in there somewhere, linking the otherwise fractured and kind of misshapen tale. It jerks, wanders, teeters from scene to scene like a film someone's edited with an ax. As in all Calhoun's dreams, people turn on him inexplicably. Sometimes they're caricatures of his family or friends. Mostly they're eerily familiar, not in physical ways, more like they know and despise him from some previous life, not that he buys reincarnation, etc. Typically, Calhoun's stumbling from a . . . say, drunken teen party to . . . some childhood memory to . . . wherever else, barely evading what feels like his imminent death. What's original here is the company. Josie's there by his side, if only half-paying attention to everything. Maybe Calhoun's trying to find them a safe place to kiss, fuck, etc., since she's nude about ninety percent of the time. Him too. In fact, hiding his bouncing hard-on from pursuers' and bystanders' eyes is a major concern every elongated and/or foreshortened second. God, things used to seem so potentially amazing re: Josie and love and all that before heroin moved in. Not that he wasn't a little distracted their whole time together, less focused on her than intent on some glorious future addiction. According to books he'd admired, heroin was supposed to make certain outdated necessities like love, friendship, sex obsolete, and it works in a way. Josie abandoned him, thanks to it. But in dreams they're "in touch" for some reason he won't understand. Because, unluckily or luckily, this brief, avantgarde, terrifyingly real seminarrative is being played out to one oblivious amnesiac, period. So it'll never be hobbled by hearsay then dashed by the embarrassing, knee-jerk, Freudianesque interpretations of listeners. It's just *his*—a little fogged-in, imaginary dart board for two minutes or something, then . . . Hey, it never even happened in the first place.

* * *

Ziggy's dry around the eyes, though, by the feel, his idiotic face isn't itself yet. Roger's probably gone, fingers crossed. Cricket could be . . . oh, anything from redoing his/her ugly makeup to, uh, throwing an antihim tantrum somewhere. Shit. His/her bedroom's not all that bizarre the more and longer he looks. It's just a sexier and less, uh, restrained relative of his Hüsker Dü shrine. Maybe this cute guy's a genius. It happens. Suppose what seems smarmy to Ziggy is actually pride in some incredible achievement? I should ask him/her, Ziggy thinks. Remember. Still, as reverential and studious as Cricket's wall-to-wall, uh, whoever shit is, Ziggy's too wrecked to buy a new, untested god at the moment. He needs something . . . familiar but really . . . spectacular. Ideally Calhoun, though two phone calls in under three hours is pushing it. And he's too . . . rattled to deal with Nicole. Shit. Drugs would help, that's for absolutely fucking sure, ha ha ha, which . . . reminds him. "Hm." Blink, blink. Picturing the miniature, powder-filled bag in his swirly, discarded jeans, Ziggy tenses a second, then, squeak, squeak, squeak, dive-bombs the boy/girl's, uh, Princess phone.

Click.

"Annie speakin'." The words are buried in music.

"Hey," Ziggy whispers. "Cool. I'm so glad you're there."

"Ziggy?"

"Yeah. Uh, you had . . . something for sale? Sorry, I'm insane. It's been weird."

Annie turns down whatever she's watching or listening to. Probably a cassette, maybe the radio, since it's too spooky and wild to be the sound track to anything, much less MTV. "Is it your dad?"

"Yeah. We're at Cricket's. You know, that transvestite from school? We *were* having a three-way until *I* freaked out."

"Ah understand," Annie says. "Well, lahk ah said on mah message, ah've got this new thang, Superchunk, named after the band. It'll flatten you out emotionally lahk you tend to enjoy. Plus it's an aphrodisiac, ahm told."

Ziggy thinks about that. "Okay, cool," he decides. "But first, about the heroin? See, like I told you, my best friend's a junkie. And I've started to think I shouldn't do it, 'cos—"

"Yeah, Calhoun," Annie says. "Nahce gah."

"Totally! But he's gotten kind of . . . too addicted now? And he's going to quit, like, tonight. So I probably shouldn't do it, out of respect."

Annie's quiet for a moment. "You wanna exchange it for somethin' else?"

"Uh, maybe." Wondering, Ziggy absentmindedly scans Cricket's room, but its furniture's dwarfed by his/her homemade wallpaper, and, now that he's sobered a little, those hundreds of flirtatious looks sort of draw him in.

"Ah'd recommend Superchunk."

"Okay." Ziggy scoots across the bed and rips a cute young guy picture away from the wall.

"Bring it to school Monday, 'kay?"

"Cool. Thanks." Up close, the guy's smarmy grin rings . . . whatchacallit . . . a bell. "But . . . Annie, uh . . . do you think I'm insane?"

"Nah."

"Me neither," Ziggy says. "Oh." He's just realized the kid in the pictures is what's-his-name . . . Shit. Arnold Schwarzenegger's little protectee in . . . what's that movie . . . *Terminator 2?* " 'Cos, uh . . . I love Calhoun," he adds, distracted.

"You should," Annie says.

"I *do.*" Ziggy crumples the picture. "Probably too much. I mean, 'cos what if he O.D.ed? I'd be so . . . fucked. Shit." Noticing what he's just done to the picture, he lays it out flat, smoothing with his palms.

"Well," Annie says. " 'Kay, you wanna know mah take on Calhoun?"

"Sure." Ziggy gives the crinkled picture a last stroke, stroke, stroke.

"Lemme read you the lyrics of this song ah wrote. It's about Calhoun, raht? And, well . . . it sorta says it all. Here, let me fahnd the thang."

"You wrote a *song* about *Calhoun?*" Ziggy slugs his knee. "Wow."

"Sure did."

"Weird. Are you in a band or something?"

"Jus' startin' one."

"What's it called?" Slug, slug, slug.

"We're called Junior High."

"Cool. What instrument do you play?"

"Drums. Ahl raht, here 'tis. Ah cain't sing, so ah'll talk it. The song's jus' tahtled 'Calhoun's Song' raht now. And it's s'posed to be kahnda hidden under lotsa guitar, so it's gonna sound nekkid, but . . . 'Kay, here goes. Um . . .

Hey boy, wake up, the police are outside
Bushes rustle with their billy clubs
Officers are bangin' on the door, boy
An' we have to git rid of the heroin

But you're not noddin' out, you O.D.ed
Cold to mah touch, no prittiness in your ahs
Ah dragged mahself out of mah nod, boy
But your hah musta killed you

Spacy angel, so smart an' unhappy
You wanted a world all your own
Ah helped, though mah heart tol' me not to
Now ahm gonna have to pay for mah kahndness

Hey boy, the police are around us
Stupid dead junkie, they're sayin'
An' ahm goin' to prison forever, boy
For the crahm of supportin' your habit

But this story ain't true, it's a message
To someone ah know who won' listen

To his friends, to the truth, to himself even

You got so much to give, boy, quit usin'.

Ziggy's pleasantly teared up. "Wow, Annie, that's
. . . great. But it's . . . pretty scary." He wipes his nose.

"Ah know." She sounds all choked up or whatever
too.

"Have you, like, read it to him?"

"Nah. Ah should, ah should. But ah don' even
know if the band's gonna go for it. It's awful corny, ah
guess."

"Yeah, but . . . Calhoun *makes* people get corny
about him, 'cos he's so, like . . . sympathetic." Ziggy flops
back on the bed, mentally building a song out of what
Annie read, plus some speed metal riffs, screechy vocals,
back-masked Satanic messages, etc. "So . . . are you in
love with him? 'Cos it . . . sounds like it. Sorry." Annie's
song's too chaotic or something, in theory at least, so
Ziggy lets it sort of skid to a halt.

"Mebbee. Ah think he's rilly sweet. But ah've got
this bad habit of goin' for gahs lahk Calhoun who're
kahnda . . . self-involved."

"Yeah, but . . . ," Ziggy says, sitting up. "He's a
great writer, and, uh . . ." He pounds his head. ". . . that's
how he has to live."

"Oh, ah know. It's jus' hard to love gahs lahk
that."

"I dig, I dig. You have to . . . have lots of, uh, faith?
My school therapist says it's like trying to be friends with
somebody who doesn't speak English. But . . ." The dam-

aged young actor's recaught Ziggy's eye. "Shit, I'd better go, Annie. I'm not at home, like I said."

" 'Kay, see ya."

Ziggy's already frantically smoothing the picture. "Uh—"

Click.

Ziggy refits the fucked-up picture into its original space on the wall and presses hard, hoping the backside's two crisp Scotch tape loops have some power left. The thing sticks, not without a few tremors. So he withdraws in extremely slow motion, diverting one hand toward the phone, even though it takes over a minute to make the stupid, half-second trip.

Click.
Ten seconds of distorted rock music.
Beep.

"Calhoun? You awake? No? It's Ziggy . . . Fuck. Okay, a little tip. You know Annie, that drug dealer girl? She likes you *a lot*. She just told me. So . . . use that info however you want, ha ha ha. Bye."

Click.

*K*en stared at his bedroom door. A nothing-special wooden rectangle. Behind it, occasional thumps, curses, moaning.

Tick, tick, tick . . .

Fatso, slumped on the couch, catatonic, insides going crazy, especially his lungs, heart.

Thud, thud, thud . . .

Rrrring. Click. "Yeah?" asked the fat man.

"It's your brother," said Brice's voice. "I'm bored. Entertain me."

Ken laid out what happened, beginning with Robin's knock-knock on the front door, ending up with the bedroom door Ken was half-studying, half-guarding.

"No shit," said Brice. "I wish I had something half as interesting to report. I . . ."

Behind the door, Frankel said something, short sentence, seven words tops. It sounded as if he was giving somebody an order, but his voice was too low to reach Ken, and not loud enough to crack a dead kid's ears, obviously.

The world was *so fucking depressing*.

"What?" asked the fat man. He'd missed something.

"I said I'm in Fullerton," Brice repeated. "With that boy I've been screwing on weekends. I'm trying to turn myself on, so we can do our little S&M number."

Across the room, a relatively silent door.

"What's his story again?" Ken asked.

"*You* remember. That son of a friend of this asshole I used to tend bar with. Prissy wanna-be model. Not bad when he *keeps his mouth shut*. Works for some clothing designer. Drinks like a *goddamned fish*."

"Someone I could . . . borrow?"

"Sure. Hey, Perry, you want to be in a porno film? Perry asks, How much will you pay him?"

"Depends. How cute is he? How young can he play? What are his limits?"

"Oh, he's cute, all right. Could pass for maybe . . . seventeen? But he's twenty-two, I think. Wait. Hey, my brother wants to know what your limits are? Hey, Perry, reality's calling. What? Forget it, Ken, he's too sloshed."

"Bring him over sometime," said the fat man. "Tell him I pay anywhere from a hundred to three hundred dollars. And he has to keep his mouth shut."

Bedroom door: Thump, thump, thump . . .

Earpiece: Tinny crash.

"*There* you go, Perry," Brice said, laughing. "He just fell flat on his face. No, *lie* there. Don't move. You look hot. I'm digging this. I don't care if you broke your wrist. He thinks he broke his wrist. I'd better say Adios, Ken. Sorry about your little problem."

"Yeah."

"Look, I'll take care of business here, head home, shower, and bring Perry over."

"Give me two hours."

Ken hung up, stared.

Bedroom door: Thump, thump, thump . . .

The fat man imagined the dead kid, then Frankel, and puzzled their bodies together, trying to make up a sex act that matched the simplistic, percussive sound track.

Not much luck.

* * *

May I note a discrepancy of sorts between the sex I'd been having with Ziggy to this point in time, and my scanty recountings? It seems I'm examining the boy at too great a remove in some ways and overwhelming him with faint praise in others.

I'll try again. Ziggy McCauley: the Tiffany of skeletons packed tightly with lush, modest musculature and flesh, etc., then enclosed in the most expensive skin ever made, which, once secured to his insides, has been treated less gingerly than it deserves, but that's teenagers for you. Now imagine something unknown is malfunctioning within this prized, somewhat scuffed body. A broken valve or two, perhaps. Such that intense smells emanate from where mild ones belong. Armpits, asshole, crotch, feet, mouth . . . Have I left someplace out? Each individual odor is tuned to the spot, so it's not as if he's been invaded exactly. More like he's turned up too high, or overextended physiologically, such that he's in that condition particular to elderly machines, when their natural stinks become . . . magnified, is the word. And during sex, one has the choice of embracing them studiously, as I did—which involves a transcendence of one's normal instincts—or resorting to very dumb acts such as mutual masturbation in order to evade these odors' not insubstantial reach. But I digress.

Ziggy's mouth: Superficially, its stench was reminiscent of anyone anywhere's "morning breath," that is, the stomach's backdraft after eight or so undisturbed

hours of breaking down food. I had learned to accommo-
date this gaseous odor long before bedding the boy, as it
impinged on our relationship in general. Through much
hard analysis, I'd managed to find its variations in detail
and strength more than slightly intriguing. There were
even some points during our sexual encounters when I
rushed at this orifice, eager to check its emission. Absurd,
I know.

Armpits: A sweetness pervaded their otherwise typical reek, particularizing them nicely. I can honestly say
that in all my erotic travails, I have never encountered a
boy anywhere whose pits housed so exotic a smell. I had
no trouble redesignating them Sirens, and resting my nos-
trils and lips there whenever physically possible. I might
add that for some unknown reason deodorant had little
effect, merely decorating their inherent charisma a bit,
not uninterestingly.

Crotch: Even freshly showered, it suggested the
genitalia of a sex maniac. The distinctive, exquisite
aroma of cooking sperm enveloped those scraggly pink
organs, more often than not blended in with a harsh un-
derodor of urine, which may have resulted from rarely
laundered garments. And on those precious occasions
when Ziggy grew sexually excited enough to reach orgasm, the blast of ulterior perfume was beyond compre-
hension.

Ass: In short, it emitted a stench I'd best leave in
absentia, or at least to the discretion of listeners, as you
would recognize this smell to which I obliquely refer from

your own, well, *experiences*. Yet I'm positive you would agree that within its rottenness was a flowering so sweet and spicy . . . a secret, addictive ingredient that made one inevitably return.

As to what was transpiring amidst this particular stretch of our story, let's see . . . I'd slunk out of the room. Ziggy's outburst had not just distressed me emotionally, it quite interfered. I'd begun to suspect my own tastes, and considering the profession I've chosen, that *just could not happen*. I was making my way toward the door when Ziggy's drag queen boyfriend grabbed my arm, and beseeched me to stay a few minutes.

We retired to the kitchen, specifically a small breakfast nook. He sat across the table, collecting himself, I suppose, while, under cover of kind, patient smiles, I did a quick critical read. Cricket would have been cute minus, oh, fifteen pounds. Far too high-strung, he was nevertheless rather bright, with a broad, pale face, and activity-fraught eyes—I'm not recalling their color—framed not unpleasantly by a spill of brown hair, albeit gone ratty by that stage.

"Is this situation confusing you?" I asked, since he was positively jittery over there.

Cricket crinkled his nose. "How," he said, taking a deep breath. ". . . *how* can you do sexual things with your *son?*"

I explained how the odd combination of Ziggy's not being a blood relative and our familial proximity had made him something of an intimate stranger to me, thereby lending his body an aesthetic importance that no other male's could potentially match.

Cricket was nodding along, but his expression seemed unconvinced.

So I changed tacks, querying Cricket as to the nature of *his* interest.

"Ziggy's cool," he said, flushing. "Everybody I know thinks so. Well, not *everybody*. The elite do, and we're the only people who matter." He grinned a fraction. "The other students are all just . . . oh, brainwashed idiots."

I detected a mild surliness in his tone, as if he wished me to glean that his pseudointellectual friends and he understood Ziggy, not I. Indeed. And I was bringing the brat back to earth when, through his evident misery, Cricket flip-flapped a hand, as if to shush me. Sure enough, we could hear someone moving our way through the building.

*C*upping his cock, balls, pubes, Ziggy follows some noise to the kitchen. Creak. The walls are beige, à la most of the rest of Cricket's parents' house, only shinier, as if wallpapered with autumn leaves, which . . . he squints . . . maybe it is. Weird. Roger and the boy/girl are studying him from this table, their bodies sidelit complicatedly by a huge, bush-clogged window.

"Goodness," says Roger. "It's the world's most perfectly formed human being." He crumples one hand several times. "Come, come."

"Hi, sorry," Ziggy mumbles, squeezing into a seat next to Cricket. He folds his hands on the table and looks at them. "When I, uh, freak out, it's never about who I'm with. It goes back to Brice. Oh, uh, he's my *other* dad. Anyway, it's all just stored-up old shit."

Roger and Cricket look tired and unreadable, especially him/her, whose makeup-smeared face and tangled hair are more Heavy Metal than girl now.

"So what've you two guys been doing?"

"Well, I've been polling your friend," Roger says. "For his assessment of you, and for the thoughts of other boys at your school."

Cricket's smiling wearily out the window.

Ziggy's hands, shoulders bunch. "I wouldn't say I'm very popular *there.*" He grabs, spins a generic-looking salt or pepper shaker.

"According to Cricket here," Roger says, watching the chess piece–like shaker whirl . . . clunk, clunk, clunk . . . "you leave most students cold, true enough, but they're . . . 'idiots,' he says, and you utterly enthrall some superior types."

"Oh, yeah?" Ziggy smirks.

"*Sure,*" Cricket says, perking up. He/she places his/her hands over Ziggy's, and hunts through his eyes with his/hers. "Don't you *know* that?" He/she blinks. "You *must.* We talk about you *all the time.* How you're *so beautiful,* but so . . . *insecure* and . . . *sweet!* That combina-

tion almost *never happens,* you know? So to us you're this
. . . *angel.* And when Nicole told us she'd *made* it with you
. . . Oh, we *flipped."*

Ziggy grins, really happy now, even if what he/she's
reporting's too weird to absorb.

"And he's *mine,"* Roger says, snickers actually, at
Cricket. "I informed our little chick-with-dick about your
immediate departure."

"Oh, that." Ziggy squeezes Cricket's hand, as, like,
reassurance or something. "That's uh . . . ha ha ha." He
glances nervously at Roger.

"You're moving to New York?" Cricket smiles
painfully at the outdoors.

Ziggy shrugs, like it's nothing to worry about.

"He *is,"* Roger tells Cricket. "You *are,"* he adds,
frowning at Ziggy.

"Maybe e-*ven*-tually." Ziggy spins the shaker
again, more haphazardly this time.

Roger and Ziggy trade glares above the shaker's
nutsy rattling around. When things get too . . . still, Ziggy
gives Cricket's small, pristine yard the once-over, though
it's more to align himself with his/her world than to seek
inner peace or whatever. "So, Cricket," he whispers.
"What're all those pictures of that *Terminator 2* kid
about?"

His/her face flushes. "I wish I knew. I'm in love
with him, I guess."

Ziggy literally has to bite his bottom lip to kill a

huge, ugly grin. "Isn't the guy, like, thirteen years old or something?"

"So?" Cricket winces. His/her eyes are sort of teared-up and glary. "I'm never going to meet him anyway."

"But . . . he's just a piece of paper."

"*I* know." He/she half-tips, half-slumps sideways, flattening his/her face, squeak, on the windowpane. "Life's so . . . unfair." The glass clouds.

"Hey!" Ziggy pounds his forehead. "Maybe I should interview you about this. For my magazine. Except I'm not sure if it's enough about sexual abuse." Pound, pound. "I *guess* it is. I mean, it's sort of like self–sexual abuse or something, right? 'Cos, I mean, it's so impossible."

"I . . . *know*." Cricket sniffles.

Roger's been studying the pair, his eyes slitted and shiny in Ziggy's peripheral vision. "Touching," he says, easing out of the breakfast nook. "And probably a good note to close on." Pointing down at Ziggy's head, he slowly raises the finger, like he thinks he's the star of that TV show Brice is addicted to . . . what's it called . . . where a Martian lives over some woman's garage, and can move stuff around with little flicks of his digits.

Ziggy waits an interminable moment before standing up at a completely different speed from the finger's. "Don't worry," he says, eyeing Cricket's smudged, all-but-fogged-up reflection. He/she/it's started sobbing or something. Shit. "I'll, uh . . . call you tomorrow, okay?"

Cricket's dim, reflected mouth wobbles into a smile. "Promise?" he/she/it whispers.

"Promise, yeah. After"—he shoots Roger a murderous eye roll—"*he's* gone."

"*H*ello, Ziggy? It's Calhoun." He coughs. "You . . . screening your calls? I got your message. Thanks for the tip." A chuckle. "You're coming by later, right? See you then." Calhoun hangs up, and immediately flips through his phone book, hoping Ziggy's okay, though he despises worrying, so the thought sort of O.D.s. The book's blank, all except for one page where the five scattered people he . . . loves is the wrong word. Enjoys, yeah. Five tolerable people are stacked one on top of the other. Three of the numbers are dealers', one's Ziggy's, the last one's long distance. "Shit." Calhoun pokes in those once-too-familiar ten digits. Rrring, etc. Josie's deep, prerecorded voice answers. First a chillingly businesslike request to leave a message, then an almost sweet "thanks." Beep. "Josie, hey, it's Calhoun. I'm . . . sorry I haven't called in so long. I'm doing okay. You'll be happy to know I'm finally kicking heroin starting tonight. So maybe you'll call back and wish me well. Okay, see ya." He hangs up, picturing Josie's nude body, which is so dimmed by the months since he's seen her that she just sort of haunts him, rather than going directly to his crotch and/or heart. Deep breath. "All right." He calls Annie. She, of course, picks up. "Hey," he says tensely. "It's Calhoun." Annie's voice does this hop-skip-jump through several registers, though her actual words stick to hi-how's-it-going-type shit. "Why don't you come on over?" he says. "Not to sell me anything, to hang out." Annie pauses, then twangily agrees. "Is now okay? I have to do something later on." Sure, etc. "See you soon then." Calhoun hangs up and looks at his crotch, meaning a rumpled zipper and several faded blue folds. Nothing's distinguishable in that. Picturing the long-unwashed genitals inside is like finding someone you "love" drowned in a swimming pool, or so it strikes him for some drug-induced reason. He could dive in and go through the motions of resuscitating whoever, but what's the use? Maybe they're better off dead. Maybe Annie can do something. Imagining her head on his lap making labored attempts, he reaches into his desk drawer and fishes out a glossy packet of heroin. He pours a bit onto a spoon, adds water, and fires up the lighter beneath. Sniffle. It's . . . ready. Annie faded out two or three seconds ago. Okay, which needle? "You." Tick, tick, tick, tick . . . Maybe his eyes got too close to the fumes or . . . whatever, but, tying his upper arm, everything suddenly seems so . . . difficult, not just to watch, to process, and by the time a remotely accessible vein fends its way through the bloat in one trembling hand, tears have really, indiscriminately gathered. "Shit," he croaks. Calhoun can't see.

*   *   *

Ken sat rewinding the Robin porn.

Background, a running bath. Tick, tick, tick . . .

"Shit." He walked into his bedroom, absentmind-edly clutching the TV's remote control unit.

Stiff kid, hanging off the bed, butt sculpted into a misshapen basin, cute face squashed flat as a boxer's, arms fallen hither and thither, legs splayed unrealistically wide across the disheveled bedding.

Rigor mortis, weird.

Ugly sugary smell from Robin's basic direction.

Ken, trying to fill in a narrative.

He edged over, pinched his nose, peering down into Robin's new asshole.

Behind the fat man, subtle toweling sounds.

"Thanks again," said Frankel. "Sincerely."

Ken nodded, hypnotized.

Tick, tick, tick . . .

Frankel moved to Ken's right, watching, toweling. "Mm *mm*," he joked. "I've been there."

If the kid was alive, moaning . . . If this was Cal-houn, maybe . . . As is, the fat man felt less and less horny each second.

Tick, tick, tick . . .

For whatever reason the corpse ended up on Ken's floor. Some kind of strange, avalanchelike commotion.

Thunk.

Robin, a toppled statue named Agony or some-thing.

"Too bad they rot away," Frankel said. "I'd take him home." He pulled the bath towel taut, snapped at the statue. "Have a few friends over."

Ken snorted.

"No, seriously. I think I'm in love." He aimed, snapped.

"With what?" asked the fat man. He pointed. *"That?"*

Frankel looked . . . how to put it? "Long story," he said.

"You did this . . ."—Ken waved generally at the statue—". . . before?"

"Once."

"Same situation?"

"Quite similar." Frankel sat on the bed, eyeing Robin impassively. "Friend of my son Ron's. Drugged out, long-haired mess. Cuter than this baby. Used to come around, even when Ron wasn't home. Talked to him, took him seriously. Bright kid. Deep emotional problems. Came by one night full of tranquilizers. Couldn't walk, couldn't talk. Don't know how he got there. Helped him into the guest room. Said, Sleep it off. Came back to check up a few hours later. Kid was dead. No question about it. Ron was over at Peggy's, his girlfriend. Figured nobody knew where the druggie kid was. Loner type, few friends. Even Ron was fed up with his bullshit by then. To me he was interesting. Different standards, I guess. So I thought, What the hell. Stripped him, did a heavy little number. Beautiful, *beautiful* ass. Loved how immobile it was. You can mold a dead body. Move the muscles around, they get stuck. Had an incredible time. Made him into a monster. But his smell got bad. So I buried him in the backyard. Police never came around. Never heard anything. Never stopped thinking about him. Still can't. Thought this might clear the air. Maybe it will. Definitely have a better sense of the experience now."

Ken had been listening, studying the statue too. "Yeah," he mumbled.

"Human brains are amazing." Frankel was up on his feet getting dressed in fast motion.

"So I should *bury* him?"

Frankel straightened the scarf in his breast pocket. "I honestly would take him with me, but . . ."

Reality, weird.

Down below, Robin's corpse smelled like an oven with something grotesque being cooked at a low heat inside it.

Frankel paused, staring off at some nowhere. "You want to know the difference between Ron's friend and him?" he said, blinking. "I knew Ron's friend. Built my interest up over a year. He wasn't just cute, he had meaning, you understand? I knew who was dead. I *knew* something was missing. This situation here . . . is more . . . technical."

"Maybe I didn't know what's-his-name long enough," Ken said.

"You're a fortunate man."

Frankel whipped out his checkbook.

＊　＊　＊

*B*y the time we reached Brice's, I'd given up trying to change Ziggy's mind re: the move to New York.
Truth be told, I had soured a bit on the idea myself.
Strange how repressed lust can doctor, retouch, etc., some
nice-looking nobody. Mine had virtually deified Ziggy
when, as became more apparent each minute, his beauty
came with uncontrollable contents. Still, while that surface remained both intact and available, I was pleased,
nay, honored to partake. So I ordered him onto the futon.

It was perhaps, oh, twenty-five minutes later—by
which time I'd become quite a foul piece of work, I don't
mind telling you—that I was startled to hear my son's
voice. (Just to show you how anonymous the sex felt, I
thought for a moment, What's Ziggy doing here?) He said
something about a . . . "cavern" supposedly hidden away
in his buttocks. Had I discovered it yet? he wondered.

Of course he meant his rectum, I answered, and,
yes, I'd grown familiar with its existence at least.

He seemed enthralled. What's it for? he wanted to
know. Did everyone have one? Charming.

"Your fecal material collects there," I said, and dug
two, perhaps three fingers into his ass, deep enough that
I could bend their very tips and explore the rectum's
slippery walls. "And when there's enough shit," I con-
tinued, "it weighs on the tube, and . . . time for your
toilet."

"What's in there right now?" Ziggy asked between

winces and nips at his bottom lip. Brice's bedroom had
started to smell like an extension of his bowels. Or like
. . . their museum.

I dug, dug. "Mucus," I said. "And some mysterious
seaweedy objects. It's quite hot in here. You must have a
slight temperature, but then I'm no G.P., of course."
Perhaps I found other things, I can't remember. Chiefly,
I was stunned by the ease with which his ass had accepted
my digits. "Indulge me, Ziggy," I said. Then I gently
explained the term *fist-fucking*, and asked his permission
to try this miraculous feat then and there, with a respectful narration, of course. (I know I'm speeding up.
Pardon.)

"You won't, like, destroy anything?" he asked.

Reassuring him that I wouldn't—though, as we all
know, life is guarantee-free—I bounded to my suitcase,
withdrew the tube of lubricant, and beautified my right
hand, while Ziggy watched and swallowed in my peripheral vision. It seemed nigh impossible that my nonpetite
paw could start wearing his hardly palatial young ass, yet,
once I'd rejoined the fair creature and unsealed his crack,
the anus positively yawned. Fixing my eyes on that too-
trusting face—meaning approximately half, as it was
lying on its side in a pillow—I squeezed the tube's goo
down his maw, and started punching inside.

Ziggy yelped, tensed his body, and let out this un-
forgettable scream that sounded ten miles away.

Four fingers sank almost immediately, and I was
wedging my thumb into that slobbery knothole as well,
when Ziggy lifted his head, which, I might add, was un-

pleasantly obscured by a thick, beaded curtain of sweat. "Oh fuck," said his voice. "Listen."

"Just . . . one . . . more . . . inch." (Have I mentioned that I was also masturbating this entire time?)

"No, *listen.*" Ziggy reached back and clutched at the wrist that was seconds away from immersion.

Ziggy forces his bedroom door shut, steps around busted things, and starts hurling on any old clothes he can find, no matter how wrinkled and sour.

Roger's snatched an old Hüsker Dü shirt from the floor and is toweling lubricant, shit, etc., off his hand.

Tick, tick tick . . .

"Fuck, it's hopeless." Ziggy plops on the bed, looking worriedly down his misfastened and inside-out shirt. "Okay, uh . . . we're gonna tell Brice you're visiting. Uh, and I let you crash in his room."

Roger nods. "That sounds reasonable, but—"

"Wait, wait." Ziggy slaps a fingertip to his lips. There's a racket about, say, the distance away of Brice's room, which isn't *so* dangerous, but, fuck, it suddenly mutates into the creaking that always precedes a grand entrance.

"Where do I hide this?" Roger's shaking the shirt around. "Ziggy?"

"Over . . ." Creak, creak, creak . . . "Shit! *Anywhere, Dad.*"

The door blasts open, sproing, knocks a fried egg–

sized hole in the wall, then swings into Ziggy's room,
vibrating. Enter Brice. He's dressed up in his much, much
too tight leather jacket and pants that, to Ziggy at least,
always sort of soften his scariness, or make it seem more,
like, preplanned, give it guidelines or whatever, assuming
the stuff Uncle Ken used to say about S&M being a harm-
less if X-rated sport still applies. Here's hoping. "I want
an explanation from *him*," Brice says, indicating Roger,
who's hunched way over, covering his crotch with the
T-shirt. "And *you*," meaning Ziggy, no doubt, although
Brice doesn't look. ". . . *you shut fucking up.*"

Roger's stumbling backwards. "Well . . ." He peers
at Ziggy, who can't seem to make his eyes say anything
in particular, apart from whatever they naturally exude,
which, the school therapist tells him, is neediness, period.
"The . . . explanation is . . .," he says, garbage breaking,
crunching, etc., under his footsteps. ". . . that . . . I'm in
town from New York on some business, and . . . I needed
a pit stop."

Brice's face grows a smidgen more purple and taut.
"So why does it smell like somebody's just taken a dump
in my bedroom?"

Roger shakes his head. "I really don't know."

"Here too." Brice sniffs the air right in front of his
face, then cranes his neck, inhaling dramatically nearer
Roger. "It's coming from you."

"I ate something that didn't agree with me," says
Roger. "I was about to step into the shower in fact."

Brice glares at Ziggy, Roger, Ziggy, Roger. "You're

fucking." He runs a hand through his greasy red hair, which has gone kind of Bozo in all the commotion.

Roger opens his mouth.

"Thing is," Brice adds, studying Roger. "That's a perfectly good explanation. Everyone wants to fuck Ziggy. Not just assholes like us. Women. Even a couple of straight guys I know."

Roger glances at Ziggy, brows arched, possibly to mean, Hey, the guy's not a creep after all, but their contact's too quick, and Ziggy's too physically fucked up in general, to counteract that with a knowledgeable grimace.

"So, with *that* out in the open . . ." Brice grins, for whatever it's worth.

Ziggy extends an arm. "Dad," he squeaks, paddling the air between him and Roger. "Don't believe—"

"*Shut up!*" Brice yells. "I *mean* it." He glances at Roger. "Ziggy pulls this emotional crappola *every fucking day.*"

"Whatever," Ziggy mumbles. He's begun studying a wall. Weird. Used to be he could count on it. Well, not *it* exactly, the posters. They'd beckon to him in a way. Not that any one member of Hüsker Dü ever looked enviably happy, but something about those three older guys' eyes, and the misery they housed, did this great, corrective thing to the world. It seemed roomier or something. More . . . uncharted. They knew a spot. Somewhere realistically bizarre, not just overly imagined on drugs then transcribed in corny outer-space colors, like on the posters that spaced out most kids he'd grown up with. It would've been cool to see Bob Mould, Grant Hart, and . . . uh . . . what's-his-name at the moment, instead of just whitish, depressing rectangles. "Dad?" Ziggy says, shivering a little. "I've got some heroin in my jeans pocket. Can one of you get it out for me? 'Cos I think I'm going to cry."

Brice squats and starts fishing around in the crumpled jeans, which are so long unlaundered that Ziggy can smell their ancient piss stains from here. "This?" he asks, holding up the Baggie.

"Yeah. And there's a straw in the pocket too." Tick, tick, tick . . . Ziggy's handed the stash. A straw's jabbed between two of his fingers. He gets to his feet, pretty shakily, duh, and stumbles over to the last of the room's decorations, a mirror. He lifts it off its cobwebby hook. Avoiding eye contact with anyone, he carries the thing to his bed, sits. Balancing this silvery sheen on his knees, he makes up two huge, chalky lines of the heroin, raises the mirror almost to his face, and snorts everything away. Now he can see a distorted reflection of Roger and Brice. They're either hugging or wrestling each other. Weird. Sniffling, Ziggy throws the mirror down on the floor, where it basically blends in with the other ruined bullshit. Still, he can see a little bit of himself. He looks overweight, thanks to the angle, not to mention thanks tons to the heroin. It's making everything fuzzy. Him too, or . . . warm's better, yeah. Improved. Him, his dads, their poses, his thoughts . . . But, uh, something, like, shifts—

he can't tell in which direction at first—and a chill trickles into the warmth, tainting it, then—whoa—completely polluting him. He's ice cold. "Oh, fu-u-u-ck," he moans, remembering. "I'm going to throw up. I . . . forgot that's what . . . happens." He sort of writhes to his feet in slow motion. "Shit, I need to . . . get to the . . . bathroom." He stumbles a few inches. "Don't worry. I'll be . . . okay." Run, he thinks. Door. The hallway weaves, rocks precariously below him.

*R*obin's . . . whatever oozed out of his nose. Overhead, leafy tree limbs swayed around, interrupting the pale moonlight shimmer on him.

In the corner of Ken's eye, the body kept reanimating. Hands twitched, eyes blinked, etc. He had to keep freezing his shovel in midair to check.

"Phew."

Fat, wet, reeking, breathless silhouette bending way over, straightening up, bending way over . . .

Chunky dirt piling up next to a ditch.

Distant barking pet dog for several nerve-racking seconds.

A corpse titled Robin, definitely not the young cutie he may or may not have been once. Hard to remember now.

Ken tried to be even more mechanical. Up, down, up, down . . .

Then he walked into the house, popped a beer, came outside, set the cold bottle far enough away from the digging that dust couldn't filter inside.

Robin's soul or whatever way off in . . . wherever death was, probably nowhere.

At some point the fat man sat down on a lawn chair. "Five minutes." He wheezed.

And the sweat started chugging out.

Night sounded distant and soft.

Robin, flat on the ground, so fucking lost, like a kid in a "dead body" Halloween costume, but worse, more realistic, not endearing at all.

Ken spaced out on the body a while.

Faintly off in the house: Rrring, rrring, rrring, click, "This is Ken's phone machine. Leave a short message," beep, "Ken. It's Brice. I'm running late. I told Perry we'd meet at your place. So if he gets there before me, have fun."

How great to put an old-fashioned picture frame around everything from this moment on.

"I can't think," said the fat man.

Ken labored up to his feet, using the mud-caked shovel as a crutch.

Over to the left, Robin the nothing.

*C*alhoun and Annie are seated on his double bed, shooting up side by side. He talked her into it, even though she'd been clean for a month, all of which is extremely romantic to his mind. They settle back, nodding. He opens his eyes on occasion and watches her head bob, eyelids flutter. That's sexy, he doesn't know why. When their rushes dim down, he starts kissing her. Clothes off, they fuck, which is surprisingly easy on heroin. It's impossible to come, if you're a male, which helps Calhoun concentrate. After a few minutes, Annie makes a discomfitted face, jolts, relaxes, meaning he's been a decent lay. They lie around together, not saying much. He switches on the TV. Some old *Married . . . with Children* rerun. During a station break, Annie asks if he's giving up heroin tonight. He says he's not sure anymore. It made sense when he said so to Ziggy, but now . . . She looks worried. That pisses him off, and he turns up the TV. Why not? she asks. Calhoun says he's not ready. There's more to be learned. If Ziggy's disappointed that's not Calhoun's problem. Ziggy doesn't know shit about heroin. Calhoun doesn't want friends. People suck. Besides, who's *she* to talk? I don't know, she says, hugging her knees. Calhoun shuts up. They watch the rerun in silence. He's hurt her. He's sorry. He can't apologize. It's just not in his nature. Please leave, he thinks. That's the easiest solution. He starts flipping the channels. She stares off. He's so tense he goes over and sits at his desk, debates a moment, then does a shot. A magnificent one. Back in bed, Annie says she should probably go. That sounds tentative. But Calhoun's nodding so heavily and nothing else matters. She gets dressed. Occasionally he opens his eyes and sort of watches her. He doesn't know what he wants. Annie walks to the doorway, turns around, and tells Calhoun she really, really cares about him. He hates all emotion and can't meet her eyes anymore. So she leaves. Slam. He lowers down on the bed, lets his nod loose again. Calhoun's mouth's dangling open, eyes basically shut. TV blares in the background. All those actors and actresses yelling dumb, memorized lines to prerecorded approval. God, Calhoun thinks, half-listening. That's the stupidest . . . sound . . . in . . . the . . . world.

Ziggy's crumpled over a toilet seat, heaving whatever the fuck's in his stomach. A thin, sour soup of ex-food, beer, saliva, etc., squirts through his trembly lips and bared teeth. His clothes are soaked through with sweat. Underneath he's incredibly fragile and blanched, a snowboy. His melty face dangles over a marbled, unfocused puddle, which rumples wildly whenever he breathes. "Shit, Calhoun," he says, and gags from the effort of focusing on something. *Hurry, pal,* answers a scratchy voice. *I need you.* As soon as I'm . . . less nauseous, Ziggy thinks, gasping. He tries to grin, which makes his throat hurt. Like Calhoun could read his mind anyway, although they *are* supernaturally tuned to each other, right? Probably now more than ever, since he finally understands what Calhoun's been addicted to. It definitely helps to picture him and his best friend in simul-

taneous, nearly identical poses across this huge city, each
of them sort of gargling the other's first name in a crushed,
hopeful voice. In fact . . . Ziggy blinks . . . that might, uh,
translate into a really great drawing or two. Like in *I
Apologize.* "Hm." He manages to raise his head, jiggling,
to an odorless point inches over the john. Separate por-
traits on two facing pages, he thinks. Two thin, contorted,
ineptly drawn figures, one blond, one brunette, looking
painfully in each other's direction across the magazine's
seam, both their heads crowned by, like, a trio of puffy
cloudettes that curve up to a huge, mutual thought bal-
loon/cloud that contains the words, uh . . . uh . . . "Shit."
Ziggy's head plummets into the bowl, his forehead accidentally clipping the edge of the seat, ouch, which . . . uh
. . . gives his latest, scariest implosion of nausea an appropriate visual—i.e., this glimmery fogbank that eats up the
stuff in his eyesight, and makes Ziggy feel like he's vomiting in . . . outer space?

*F*irst there was a long, awkward moment of Brice
and me hugging, believe it or not, while Ziggy heaved in
the distance. Over ten or so years, my ex-boyfriend had
sagged, creased, and thickened predictably. Once a sinu-
ous, arrogant boy-man—to use an admittedly icky yet
accurate term—at thirty-seven, he bore an uncanny re-
semblance to Red Buttons—meaning, for you younger
listeners, red-headed, alcoholic-faced, smarmy, and elfin.

Nevertheless, we were suddenly engaged in preplanning an orgy, I guess you could call it. With Ziggy, mind you. For my part I can honestly say—and perhaps I've said so already—that Brice's sexual bent re: our son both intrigued and escaped me. To witness it *firsthand* . . . But let me say, I was not about to sit idly by and watch Brice cause actual harm to the boy. If necessary, in fact, I felt prepared to utilize my few physical strengths in a bodyguard fashion.

To be blunt, it was time for a change between Ziggy and me. His beauty was sans mystery by this stage, and our fitful interaction displayed the first signs of a gentrification I knew would eventually undo our relationship.

Ahem. I'm aware just how hideous this sounds. Yet there are things that transcend other things, and the very nature of transcendence leaves it impossible to justify or interpret, yes? The family unit is an inherently fascist and oddball construction—private, sacred, untrespassable, nobody's business except those involved. Still, I *can* assure you that within my and Brice's particular closed system, a strict and responsible order was being maintained. But I digress.

Let's see. The house had grown eerily silent. We trekked down the hall, to discover our half-undressed son passed out cold near a stew-filled, grotesque-smelling toilet. Brice grabbed one of Ziggy's wrists; I clutched the other. And, to make a short story shorter, we literally dragged our ward back to his room, heaved him onto the bed, and, well, did every lascivious thing you can do to a putrid and comatose male for the next, oh, half hour?

Even a superaesthete like myself must admit there are times when no preordained stance in the world can unlock a situation's importance, much less ferret out its original trigger. Here's a pristine example. Brice and I found ourselves lost in a sexual bliss of our own strange, collaborative design, even if, on the surface, our bodies enacted some rather clichéd pornographic contortions. Perhaps after all I've related to this point, you're prepared and/or willing to fill in the details. Me, I intend to retire to a place where, freed of all responsibility—moral, semantic, and otherwise—my mind can luxuriate at will in Ziggy's memory, albeit rigorously edited.

"*H*e's back," says . . . Roger's voice?

Ziggy opens his eyes all the way. Yeah. His less evil dad is, like, inches above, gazing at . . . make that right through him, in sort of the same spooky way Roger looks at concerts he's reviewing. "Hi," Ziggy says spacily. He twists his neck, surveys the unfocused room. Brice is definitely out there somewhere. In fact . . . Ziggy strains his eyes . . . *that's* him, the white thing.

"Are you one hundred percent?" Roger asks, sounding . . . what?

Ziggy feels for a pillow, finds and crushes it against his chest, curling around all that softness. "I'm good," he mumbles. Ya-aw-aw-wn. The high's so . . . preoccupying and . . . uh, heavy, that their words, his too, mostly just twinkle ineffectually against the mental mishmash.

"We've been partying with you," Roger says. A hand comes to rest on Ziggy's waist, squeezing a tender outcropping of muscle, flesh. "A little family get-together, understand?"

Ziggy thinks about answering, can't, though it's possible his eyes and/or mouth express something totally on their own.

Suddenly Brice is right there, face close enough to Ziggy's for study. It's in rapist mode—sweaty, flushed, pupils pinned, but . . . there's something . . . it seems, looks a million times more . . . accessible. Either that or heroin's a miraculous ambassador.

"What're you thinking . . . uh . . . Brice?" Ziggy asks.

"How much hotter you looked a few seconds ago," Brice says, breath all tumultuous and sweet. "When you were unconscious," he adds, then laughs. His facial features seem slightly see-through. They float there—huge, clownish, but godlike too, which makes Ziggy feel weirdly reverent and kind of . . . gentle.

"Yeah, I'm, uh . . . ," Ziggy says, swallows. He's already forgotten his sentence's point. Something about how . . . irritating he knows he can be. "Uh . . . the school therapist told me I'm manic-depressive."

"You must've been born that way," Brice says. "I tried everything. Drugs, punishment."

"Yeah . . . thanks." Ziggy smiles. Brice's head's more and more infused with this amazing allure, like it's just been exhaled by Ziggy into the air. "Sometimes, you know, I still like you a lot, Dad, 'cos . . . you're my dad.

But I always . . . know . . . uh . . ." His eyelids have started to lower. ". . . uh, that you're going to beat me up. And I hate that."

From what Ziggy can tell, Brice's eyes are teared up, but the guy's blurry head's shaking—back, forth, back, forth—so it's hard to see past all that motion.

"I heard you," Brice mumbles.

Ziggy's happy. It's drug-induced, no doubt. Still, for whatever reason, he suddenly knows, like, for sure, that a huge part of . . . sexual abuse, at least for him, is how he loves being a target for such intense feelings, expecially from someone who knows him and isn't just stupidly thinking he's cute or whatever. That's why he hasn't killed Brice, or hired a hit man like other abused-type teens do. Yeah, and that's probably also the thing that makes *I Apologize* weird, great, and makes this whole situation with Roger and Brice so . . . tolerable. He clears his throat, forces open his eyes, trying to decide if he can focus enough to request pencil, paper.

"Facedown," Brice announces. Then, with a strangely loud crack of the knee joints, the man's on his feet. Ziggy tries to look up, but the top maybe third of his dad's body's lost in this . . . grayness, probably having to do with the heroin. "My brain," says Brice's voice, ". . . is so fucking mixed up."

Ziggy slowly unbends an arm, leg, which lowers him flat. His armpits have soured again, although everything smells really sexy to him at the moment, especially his body.

"Try rimming him, Brice," Roger says in such a

clear, serious tone that it sounds kind of jokey for some reason. ". . . if you care to, that is."

Ziggy laughs into his pillow. It magnifies the sound into a honk, ha ha ha, and makes the fabric, stuffing, etc., this cozy blast furnace for three or four seconds. He reaches back, pulls his asscrack wide open, and buries his probably moronic face deep in the pillow.

Those bones crack again. Footsteps.

"It fucking *stinks*," says Brice's voice.

"Doesn't it?" Roger's voice answers. "I'm still trying to decide if that's a problem for me, or a privileged position."

"I probably ruined his bowels." Brice's voice. "I've been fucking him since he was eight."

Eight? Ziggy thinks, sending his mind on a time trip that just sort of fades out three or four years into history.

Ziggy's fingertips ache, so he shuts his ass. No one says anything. His limp, painful hands come to rest on either side of his hips. He concentrates, trying to transform his ears into microphones, put his brain on RECORD, 'cos, obviously, his dad's conversation's an *I Apologize* coup if there ever was one.

"Ziggy?" Roger asks. "You still there?"

"Yeah, keep talking," Ziggy mumbles. He looks over a shoulder. Blur. "Both of you. It's . . . interesting."

"I just said everything," Brice says.

"Okay, uh . . ." Anyway, Ziggy couldn't move a pencil right now if he needed to. He lets his head flop on the pillow.

"We're both rather tired, dear," Roger says. "Personally, I wouldn't mind one more quick session, however. Then we'll leave you alone. Promise.''

A finger worms down Ziggy's ass, which feels . . . different than usual . . . simpler bordering on good. Still, he sucks a wad of air through his teeth in surprise. The finger moves around quickly and slides out. That *does* sting a little. There's a sniffing sound. "The smell," Roger says, probably for Brice's benefit, ". . . is far more curious concentrated on this than it is all dispersed in the air." He sniffs again. "It's nastier, but more specific. Less . . . censored. I mean, it's *who* our boy *is*. Do you know what I'm saying?''

Brice snorts.

"Hm. Are you . . . implying that Ziggy's less fascinating the better you know him?" Roger asks.

"Gotta be." Snort.

"And yet I *know* his downfalls, *know* how manipulative he is.''

Ziggy clears his throat. "The school therapist," he croaks, then hocks up some noise-goo and swallows it. "She told me I'm so fucked up now by my psycho upbringing, and, uh, the molestations and stuff, that my whole personality's, like, about using other people. 'Cos I never thought anyone would, uh, love me if I was just, like, myself?''

"You're a disaster." Roger's wagging his head. "It's fascinating.''

"Yeah," Ziggy says.

"It enriches your beauty so much.''

"Yeah, I guess." Ziggy scrunches his forehead. "To

you anyway. But . . . what do *you* think, uh, Brice?"
Hoping to see that dad better, he props himself up on his
elbows. The effort so taxes his brain that the bedroom
completely fogs over, swallowing his dads along with it,
not unlike all the dry ice, etc., that blankets less talented
rock bands in concert.

Brice's voice sort of feedbacks.

"Can you say that again?" Ziggy asks, blinking.
"I'm fucked up."

"I said I'm late for an appointment."

"Oh yeah, me too." Ziggy nods furiously, which
smokes up the room even more. Shit.

Brice snorts. Crack, crack. By the sound of it, he's
on his feet, probably leaving the premises.

"Actually . . . ," says Roger. He sounds like he's
back in his favorite locale again. *"Here's* something interesting. Your rectum smells like there's sugar inside it." A
sniff. "Do you eat a lot of carbohydrates?"

"I don't eat a lot of anything."

Down the hall, Brice's door slams.

Deep in Ziggy's ass there's this sudden, weird
stinging.

"I *really* have to *go,*" Ziggy says, grimacing. He
twists around, squints, trying to locate his dad, who's
. . . hunched way over, yeah, one, uh, hand digging around
in his . . . cavern, like someone who's dropped some car
keys into a ditch or whatever. "Uh . . . Dad!"

Roger . . . shakes his head? "One . . . ," he mumbles,
"more . . . second."

* * *

*D*ead kid not exactly snuggled up in a ditch nowhere near six feet deep.

Ken stood at the rim, reeking. "I should say something," he huffed-puffed.

Heavy Metaler's mind way, way, way beyond the white tunnel's far end, if he ever even saw that fucking myth in the first place.

Tick, tick, tick . . .

"He'd want . . . something . . . Satanic."

Robin, not necessarily anyone. A human-shaped grayness. A jellyish smell that belonged to being dead in a general way.

"Enjoy hell," Ken said, hoping that caught Slayer's drift. But he really didn't care all that much, of course.

Weird how one flinched at throwing dirt on something totally inanimate just because it was human once.

Still . . .

A hole filling up and taking with it the world's cutest Slayer fanatic.

The fat man ached every-fucking-where.

Digging, etc.

Tick, tick, tick . . .

"Hello?" Someone was clawing through bushes along the right side of the house.

"Who's there?" Ken asked, his eyes focusing on . . . Perry, presumably.

Perry: baseball cap, sideburns, tall, thin, pale, loosely dressed, flask in one hand, cigarette in the other, weaving.

Pretty kid, no ambiguity about it, though too old to unravel the fat man, except theoretically.

"Hi," Perry said. He leaned over the hole, peering down.

"My dog died," Ken said.

Ha, ha, ha . . .

The kid, obviously drunk, laughing too, though he couldn't know why or even care, thank God.

Now an awkward little not-really-sure-what-to-say-next-type moment.

The fat man studied the kid, in particular the seat of his pants, although nothing much showed, feeling more and more . . . impressed.

"Shall we . . . ?" Ken glanced at the house.

Perry smirked.

They headed off.

Imagination, weird.

*C*alhoun feels a million times better now. No hallucinations this nod, but at least the real world, and more specifically today, has settled back in its usual, meaningless place. What's happened so far forms a structure. Phone calls, visits, shots, a little sex, some TV. What's ahead seems predictable. Ziggy, his greatest admirer, will show up ere long, sit around on the fringes, exuding ridiculous amounts of affection, which Calhoun can then take or leave depending on . . . whatever. Whim? Company's cool when it's that set in stone. Annie . . . she'll come back around, or she won't. Now *there's* a nice little mystery, an interesting imaginative exercise. Not giving a fuck about sex is so beautiful. He'll have to remember to talk about this state of mind in his novel, wherever it is. Over there somewhere. Calhoun opens his eyes a slit. Yeah, that's it. That glimmering rectangular blueness, that spooky night light. "Mm . . ." What can anyone say? Calhoun's just part and parcel of the bed, an inanimate, pillowlike object, to his way of thinking. He's mere consciousness or whatever. Weird how spectacular beds are. O, to be a piece of furniture, as poets might say. In other words, to be nothing in particular and have a wild, analytical brain like his own. Hm. Calhoun's mouth, which has been hanging far open, albeit crookedly, warped by a crease in the pillow, closes slightly and . . . smirks? That's his guess. There's a very dull breeze on his bare back and ass. From where? An open door? Shit. "Hel-lo?" he asks, voice very rumbly. "Um . . . Ziggy?" But the only answer is ambience. A clock's tick, the simple buzzing in his trumpet ears. Time to zone, drift, probably in sleep's direction. "Mm . . ." When he nods, Calhoun's *this* close to invulnerable. Knives could carve, bullets lodge, cocks could plug in, loyal friends could decide to turn permanently away, bored and/or scared shitless. He'd survive, see. Peacefulness, that's what he's after, whatever the form. And heroin's sedation will do for the moment, although it wouldn't be totally obnoxious if Ziggy or someone telephoned or came by on occasion to radiate humanesque warmth. Just a teeny little bit, he thinks. Until then . . . Calhoun feels for a blanket.

Ziggy, barefoot, shirtless, torso craggy with goose bumps, jabs Calhoun's doorbell for the seventeenth time. *"Please,"* he says, marching speedily in place. He tries Calhoun's immediate neighbor, this nice older surfer he met once, twice.

The intercom feeds back. "What the fuck do you want?" yells a blurred voice. Shit.

"I'm here to see Calhoun. Uh, it's . . . an emergency."

Tick, tick, tick . . .

"Come *on. Please.* It's *freezing."*

Bzzzzz . . .

The former toy factory's central hallway is the slightest bit warmer, thank God, and almost visibly fogged with comforting, postpostpostcooking smells that change recognizably with every door Ziggy passes. Steak, maybe . . . tomato sauce . . . uh, fish . . .

Scuff, scuff, scuff, scuff.

The door just this side of Calhoun's is cracked a thin, yellow stripe. As Ziggy approaches, it swings wide. A jowly, unshaven, low-lit face jabs out, long blond hair flapping wildly around it. "Do you *know* what *time* it is?"

Ziggy bites his lip. "Uh . . ."

"Three twenty-five in the morning, kid."

"Yeah, well . . ." Ziggy slides his hands into his pockets. "Uh, sorry. Calhoun's, uh . . . sort of in trouble and he needs me to help out."

The neighbor's bagged, bloodshot eyes sort of sparkle, probably due to some better-not-to-know-about mental explosions or something. "That kid should learn to take care of *himself*." The door's yanked, and the hairy-backed, boxers-clad guy tromps toward Calhoun's door, fingering a key-ring. "I hardly even know him . . . and I'm expected to . . . " A key's poked in the lock. ". . . let his friends in . . . every time he's too loaded to . . ." Click. The door creaks open into the usual, badly lit living room. "You're *welcome*," the guy snaps. He turns, splits.

"Yeah, thanks," Ziggy yells after him.

Scuff, scuff, scuff.

"Calhoun?" Ziggy knocks on the bedroom door. Tick, tick . . . Nothing. "Uh, I'm entering, okay?" He turns the knob. "So . . . cover yourself." Cre-ea-ea-eak. The room is so dark Ziggy inches his feet along the floor like a newly blind guy, aimed, oh, maybe two and a half to three feet to the right of the laptop's turquoisey light, where, if his calculations are correct, you-know-who's spacing out and/or snoozing in bed. Fingers crossed. Yeah, here's . . . the . . . thing. Ziggy sits gingerly on some edge. Squeak.

"Hey," says a deep, soft voice.

"Oh, *amazing*. You're okay! I was, like, worried."
Ziggy crams his hands together and shoves this flesh lump
between his still shaky legs.

Calhoun coughs.

"Are you . . . in a lot of pain?" Through Ziggy's
chills, etc., he's beginning to feel the total, complicated
pleasure of being alone with Calhoun, partially thanks to
a faint, semisweet-smelling warmth that's been specifically tuned to his best friend's vicinity since heroin entered the picture.

Calhoun clears his throat. "Nope."

"Oh, okay." Ziggy's mildly confused what that
means. "That's, uh . . . great."

"I fucked up."

"You mean . . . like . . . with heroin?"

"Everything."

"Oh, uh . . ." Ziggy sorts frenziedly through that
word *everything* for a second. "Don't worry . . . uh . . ." He
almost, *almost* blurts out one of the worst possible things
he could say, i.e., that Calhoun's the greatest person on
earth, which, despite being unbelievably true, as far as he
knows, and a nice thing to tell someone else, at least in
theory, would almost for sure ruin the, uh . . . mood?

"Shit," Calhoun mumbles. "Maybe I should just
kill myself."

Ziggy's instantaneously as stiff and inoperable
below the neck as a carved figure. "Calhoun, I . . . don't
know what to say, you know?" He can't breathe all that
well. " 'Cos you hate it when I tell you you're great, but

. . . I just . . . think . . . you are, and, uh . . . I mean, I *know* you are." He gasps. "And you have to believe me, 'cos . . . your being alive is, like, *so important.*"

"Yeah."

"*Yeah. It is.*" Ziggy manages to disengage his bunched fingers. Phew. "And . . . when you quit heroin and stuff . . ." Gasp. ". . . there'll be all these new people you'll know, and, uh, fans of your novel who'll feel like me." He slugs his chest once, twice. "I know you don't want to be close to your friends, but . . ." Slug. That one helped. "Uh . . . but *we're* close, and that's not so horrible, right? I mean, there are things about me that annoy you, but—"

"It's not you, it's me." Calhoun clears his throat. "It's *my* problem."

"No, I know I'm, like, needy and insecure and all that bullshit. The school therapist says I'm so mentally fucked by my dad's molestations and stuff that I don't even . . . know what to do with other people, but . . . " He squints at the dark around Calhoun. "I'm trying really hard to be cool to you, 'cos . . . you make me happy, and . . . shit . . . if something happened to you I'd be *destroyed.*"

There's a second or two of that weird, uninterpretable silence, then . . . "Annie came by," Calhoun says.

"Already?" Ziggy sort of bodily defrosts in surprise. "That was quick. Did you guys . . . *do it,* ha ha ha?"

"Yeah. I made her come." Calhoun chuckles. "Or I think I did."

"Cool." Ziggy slugs his leg.

"Yup." There's this rustle, then several, like, knocks, which, as far as Ziggy can tell, is one of Calhoun's hands feeling around on the night table. "So . . . how was your father . . . and everything?" Scratch, scratch— An orangish flame lights Calhoun's face, cigarette between its lips, blue-green eyes wide, pupils pinned and sort of staticky, though that could be the lighter's reflection.

"Oh, God." Ziggy slams shut his eyes. "Well . . . we had this orgy with Brice." He cracks one lid. Calhoun's too low-lit to read. "I was passed out for most of it, but . . . *this* is cool . . ." The other lid flies open. "I really, like, studied them while they were . . . molesting me or whatever? So I can write about it in my magazine, and . . ." Ziggy gawks at his sketchy friend. ". . . Roger is *so insane*. It's *amazing*."

"How was your other dad?"

"You know, a monster." Ziggy feels himself stiffening again. "Maybe a little nicer than usual, but . . ." His facial skin's knotted horrendously, or so it feels. Shit. ". . . I, uh, don't want to . . . think about it."

"You all right?"

"Yeah, yeah. My ass hurts, but otherwise . . ."

Calhoun snorts.

"Otherwise, uh . . . Fuck." Ziggy slumps forward. "Forgive me, okay, but . . . I'm *so* glad to see you."

Calhoun inhales, exhales. The air gets tobaccoey. "Yeah," he says. Ziggy waits a few beats on the off chance his friend might elaborate, but that's dreaming, he knows, and, actually, the "yeah" was incredible enough, 'cos it had this, like, calm that can almost for sure be translated as happiness, whatever *that* involves. "Shit," Calhoun adds suddenly.

"What?"

"Oh, I was an asshole to Annie."

"But . . . how?" Ziggy scrunches up his face. "I can't imagine that."

Calhoun glares at his cigarette. "*I* don't know. The sex was fine, but . . . I hate emotion." He peeks at Ziggy. "So when she got on my back about not quitting heroin, I just . . . freaked out, I guess." Shrug.

"Yeah, well . . ." Ziggy shrugs back. "Uh, your heroin thing *is* pretty scary."

"To *you*, sure. I understand *that*. We're best friends, and you're worried. But she's a fucking junkie herself. And she doesn't even *know* me."

"I probably shouldn't tell you this," Ziggy says, and cracks an inadvertent, uh, grimace. He splays, shuts his legs bear trap–style a few times. "But I . . . snorted heroin."

"No shit." There's a whish, whish, whish. The cigarette's tip does a firefly zigzag through the dark. Maybe Calhoun sat up.

"It made me totally sick."

"Hm . . ." Calhoun, who, yeah, is much closer to Ziggy now, even inches away, takes a drag, blows it out. "Well, that's probably good."

"Right." Ziggy tries to get a glimpse of what little

there physically *is* of his friend. Mostly a fat, ghostly hand, skinny wrist, a minor stretch of one bruised, scabby arm. " 'Cos . . . I can inspire you to quit."

Calhoun's hand trembles, moves, plugs the cigarette in his mouth. He sucks. His tense face fades in, out.

"I mean, when you decide you *want* to quit."

Calhoun nods, then, for the next, oh, minute, smokes and makes brief dramatic appearances. Each time, his face looks a fraction less scared or pissed off or whatever. Ziggy squints in that direction, really moved, listening to Calhoun's breaths, and kind of studying the smoke he exhales, since it has the guy's being in it, however minuscule the portion. Occasionally Calhoun glances up from wherever he's looking, meets Ziggy's probably blissed if hysterical eyes, and grins for a long second.

Tick, tick, tick . . .

Calhoun clears his throat. "I should crash." He reaches out, kills off the cigarette, disappears.

"Oh, okay." Ziggy nods frenetically.

"You can stay, though. Turn on a light, if you want. It won't bother me." Calhoun, or, rather, his bed makes a few being-laid-down-on noises.

"Thanks." Ziggy slugs his knee.

"Or if you want to crash, we can share the bed. Just don't—"

"I know. *Don't try anything,* ha ha ha." Slug, slug, slug.

Calhoun chuckles. "Sorry."

"That's okay, but . . . *Really,* I don't even *want* to. It's not about sex *at all*. I—"

"I know." Calhoun clears his throat. "I'm an asshole."

"No, no, you're great. That's not what I mean. I . . . uh . . ." Shit. Ziggy's stumped. "Never mind." Still, he lets his lips silently finish the sentence, although there's so much he wants to clarify, and every possible word he could use seems so clunky, etc., that it's more like he's mouthing some prewritten, incomprehensible prayer which has nothing to do with how weird he feels while he's pronouncing it.

"Well, good night then." Calhoun . . . rolls over?

"Yeah," Ziggy whispers. "Sleep . . . tight."

Calhoun yawns.

Ziggy's getting so, like, emotional he can't think.

Tick, tick, tick . . .

Fuck everything else.